FOR LIESA AND SEAN

Glory

Forget Me Not

jodi lynn

PUFFIN BOOKS

All quoted materials in this work were created by the author.
Any resemblance to existing works is accidental.

Forget Me Not

PUFFIN BOOKS
Published by Penguin Group
Penguin Young Readers Group,
345 Hudson Street, New York, New York 10014, U.S.A.
Penguin Books Ltd, 80 Strand, London WC2R 0RL, England
Penguin Books Australia Ltd, 250 Camberwell Road, Camberwell, Victoria 3124, Australia
Penguin Books Canada Ltd, 10 Alcorn Avenue, Toronto, Ontario, Canada M4V 3B2
Penguin Books (N.Z.) Ltd, 182-190 Wairau Road, Auckland 10, New Zealand

Published by Puffin Books,
a division of Penguin Young Readers Group, 2003

1 3 5 7 9 10 8 6 4 2

Copyright © 2003 17th Street Productions, an Alloy, Inc. company
All rights reserved

Front cover photography copyright © Barry Marcus

Produced by 17th Street Productions,
an Alloy, Inc. company
151 West 26th Street
New York, NY 10001

17th Street Productions and associated logos
are trademarks and/or registered trademarks of Alloy, Inc.

LIBRARY OF CONGRESS CATALOGING-IN-PUBLICATION DATA

Lynn, Jodi.
Forget me not / by Jodi Lynn
p. cm. – (Glory ; 4)
Sequel to: Blue girl.
Summary: Still struggling with guilt and illness and missing her family in West Virginia, Glory must
decide whether or not to stay with her foster family in Boston or spend her remaining days somewhere else.
ISBN 0-14-250046-1
[1. Family—Fiction. 2. Self-perception—Fiction. 3. Foster home care—Fiction.
4. Sick—Fiction. 5. Boston (Mass.)—Fiction.] I. Title.
PZ7.L9945Fo 2003 [Fic]—dc21 2003046504

Printed in the United States of America

PROLOGUE

I know there's no point, but I keep thinking about going back in time. I close my eyes long enough to wish every terrible thing that's happened away. I keep feeling like if I only wish hard enough, I can do it—I can go back home.

I used to daydream about this stuff—going back in time—in a whole different way. I used to lie on my bed in the home where I grew up, in the small town of Dogwood, and think about heading back to ancient Egypt, or to Jesus' time. I could spend hours on my back, staring at the ceiling, dreaming of places I'd never see and people I'd never get to meet, even if I ever did leave Dogwood. But now I just dream myself back there to that spot on my bed, where everything was simple. I dream I'm that girl who liked to imagine where life might take her, still. But I'm not that girl anymore. I'm the girl who wishes she were where she used to be.

I'd even settle for the time *after* Dogwood. Even after my best friend Katie and my family and home were gone and I was miserable and sad and living in a barn in a stranger's backyard. Or even afterward, living with Becky Aiden and her family in

Shadow Tree, working at Becky's store to save money for my bus ride to Boston. Maybe it's just because I miss Becky and her family, from time to time. And Jake. But I also think it's because part of my brain believes that staying in one place would have somehow stopped time from speeding forward and bringing me here, to the brink of the end.

But of course I know that's not the way it works. Time moves forward no matter where you plant your feet. My time would be running out, anywhere on this planet. And instead of running out in Becky's town, Shadow Tree, it's running out here, in Boston. It's as simple as that.

Only, I never expected it to be running out so quickly. It's been four months since I arrived here, but it seems like weeks. The things that have happened to me since then—meeting my foster parents, going to a big, modern school, getting to know Joe and then ending the friendship—all seem to smush together in my brain like peas in a pod, but when I stop to think about it, I know they are stretched apart by days and days and days.

How long do I have left? One month, two? Can I make it to Christmas? Now that I've got modern doctors poking and prodding me, I suppose it's possible. I have the tiniest sliver of hope, which—a couple of weeks ago—was not there at all. But compared to that sliver is the memory of what the Reverend said—

that I'd have a year at most, if I was very lucky. And that modern doctors wouldn't be able to help. And then, there's the fact that I've gotten so ill already.

One thing I know for sure is that time is not gonna come back for me. No matter how hard I wish or dream or think about it. I've started to see home the same way I used to see places in storybooks, as beautiful and perfect, and so far away it feels almost imaginary. I can see the outlines of it in my head— the houses and the mountains and the leaves in autumn; I can see the shed and the church and the folks. I can see Katie, with her colt legs and her perfect chestnut hair, doing all the things that made her my best friend—like listening to me, and laughing with me, and being there. But I'm starting to forget the smells, and the feeling of my mama's hug. I can see Katie's hand, but I can't remember what it felt like holding mine. I even forget just what my daddy's voice sounds like. I can see the shed on Christmas Eve, and the case of wine—I never stop seeing that. But it seems like somebody else is there, getting Katie to drink. I can see the icy lake, the one that stole Katie's life away, all because of my mistake. But Katie and me on that lake are like paper dolls—we're too small to be real.

It's frightful, to have all of these thoughts and memories leak out of my brain and drift off into nothing. But to tell you the truth, I'm glad of it, too. Because I'd like to have some peace, before I fade off into nothing myself.

Sure, I guess I could at least *hope* for better things—to survive, like my foster parents say I will, or to go to heaven or to get forgiveness for what I did back in Dogwood that night. Folks at home would certainly tell me to repent so that the Lord might save me. But I don't believe in getting saved anymore—not that way. Anyway, if God is up there at all, then surely He's meant me for other things. Back home, the Reverend always talked about hellfire, and if there is such a place I suppose I'm meant for that.

But I've come to think, if God were really in charge, why would He have taken Katie away? Why would He let so many bad things happen? The way I see it, there's nobody like that looking out for me, anywhere—above or below. I figure when I die, I'll just be asleep, and I'll have nothing and be nothing and feel nothing at all.

And it seems to me that isn't all bad. Because then never again will I think of Katie, and how she's sleeping, too, because of me.

The doctors say that they can help. The Kellys know all about my punishment now, and how it's poisoning me. They say we just have to find out the problems it's causing in my body, and fix them. And I guess I hope they're right. But what if they are? Then I don't get to forget, I don't get to sleep.

And then, what if they aren't? What if these are my last months in the world, like I've believed ever since I left home? What if my time stops, and I—Glory Mason—simply fade away?

CHAPTER ONE

Snip. Snip snip.

"How's it going out there?"

Snip.

Pinching a bundle of fat green rose stems between my left thumb and forefinger, I turned to stare at my foster father, Mr. Kelly. He was standing in the back doorway of the house behind me, the walls of which were almost the exact same color as today's sky. For a moment, squinting, I couldn't see where the outline of one ended and the other began.

"Fine, Mr. Kelly." My voice came out warm.

Mr. Kelly raised his eyebrows, acknowledging my good mood. It hadn't been long since we'd all been angry and upset and hiding things from one another—back before I told them about the poison, back when Katie's daddy had found me downtown and sent me home with bruises and no answers. Boy, things had changed.

The secret of the Water of Judgment was out in the open, and instead of being the disaster I'd feared, it had changed everything for the better. Suddenly there was this whole wave of trust running back and forth between the Kellys and me—despite the things I still insisted on keeping to myself (like why I'd been punished in the first place). We had lots of days like this now, where we felt at peace with one another, instead of nervous. Back home, there'd been a song we sang in church about harmony, and this seemed to be what it was like. It was nice.

What's more, instead of being heartbroken over my news about the poison, the Kellys had sworn up and down that everything was going to be all right—that they were going to get me healthy again. At least, Mrs. Kelly had. Mr. Kelly had nodded, or said "absolutely," or given me these kind, awkward pats on the back to say he felt the same.

So instead of me causing them hurt, they'd lifted my hopes. Even though, so far, all the doctors had done was stick me with needles and talk about all these "tests" they had to do, and then shake their heads when the tests didn't tell them anything helpful about my illness.

Through it all, the Kellys had kept cheerful, saying the next set of tests, or the next visit, would surely bring good news. And I suppose that was why I felt cheerful, too.

From where he stood in the doorway, Mr. Kelly turned his head and called back into the kitchen, "I believe she's turning into a real gardener." A figure behind the window—Mrs. Kelly—nodded agreement.

I put a hand to either side of my broad straw hat self-consciously, tugging at it to make sure it was on straight. Then I looked down at my hands, tucked tightly into Mrs. Kelly's small pink suede gardeners. On my feet were Mr. Kelly's green rubber Wellingtons, which my foster parents had bought on a trip to some faraway place like England, or Alaska, or some-place. I sure *looked* like a real gardener.

My daddy would have bust a gut seeing me like this— trussed up like a turkey for something as simple as trimming a bunch of flower bushes—if he didn't die first from the shock at seeing me do it of my own free will. Once, gardening was the worst form of punishment the town folks could think to give me for all my troublemaking—which, of course, seems silly now. But who would have thought I might actually turn out to like it someday? And that it would bring me comfort by keeping my mind off the worse punishments that had come along?

I pushed the thought out of my mind. My stomach felt a bit achy today, but not a sick kind of ache. It felt like maybe I'd stretched my muscles too far while I was leaning over gardening. I rubbed at my belly, then lifted the shears in my right hand and went back to work.

Mrs. Kelly had entrusted me with deadheading the roses, which was a job that went like this: If the edges of the flower's petals were brown, it was a goner and had to be cut from the plant. Also, if the rose was wilted—droopy, sickly, a darker color than the fresh blossoms, it got snipped, too. Mrs. Kelly had explained how, when I found a flower that needed to be cut, I should find the closest grouping of five leaves below it, then apply a quick pressure to the scissors just above that spot, making a clean, diagonal cut through the stem. The old flower would fall to the ground and, Mrs. Kelly had said, make room for a new flower—even a whole new batch of flowers—to grow in its place.

The whole process was a little sad. Every once in a while I would have to make a tough decision about a flower that was maybe just a little brown but still had some life in it yet. I was supposed to snip these, but I always felt guilty when I did.

Still, like I said, the work gave me comfort. I loved the calm, rhythmic motion of the shears. I loved feeling like I was helping the plant grow and stay healthy by cutting out the weak bits. I wished, of course, that somebody could do the same for me.

But that was another good thing about gardening—it helped

to ease my mind. It was so simple and calming, like sleeping, or like when I used to pray. I could concentrate on it and not think about all the dark memories of Katie lying on the ice and the Water of Judgment and my family walking away from me.

Recently, the memories had gotten fainter anyhow. They were sort of like pinpricks these days—sharp and hurtful, but not unbearable like they used to be. If I stayed busy enough, I could keep them that way, it seemed. And if I watched where I let my mind go.

Now I crouched and took hold of a Blue Girl. These were my favorite of the roses, I suppose because I'd chosen them myself. They were really more light purple than blue, but the name fit. There was something so fragile and mournful about their color. The one in my hand had a yellowish brown tinge around the edges. I snipped, and it fell to the ground.

"Whew." Standing upright again, I stretched the knots out of my spine. Then I looked down at my overalls and dusted off the bits of leaves and dirt and whatnot. With my eye on my next flower, I brushed my backside, too, just for good measure.

I stopped short when my hand brushed against something wet. I ran my palm up and down once, wondering. How could it be wet? Had I sat in something?

Dumbly, I craned my head over my right shoulder, as if it

were actually possible to see your backside from that angle. There was only one person I ever knew who could turn their head that far around on their neck—Joshua Brown back home—and he'd been taken by a fit three years ago and never recovered.

Finally I had the better idea of running up to the Kellys' room. They had a full-length mirror the likes of which I hadn't seen until coming to live with them—with gilded edges and glass as clear as crystal. I walked past Mr. Kelly, sitting in the kitchen, and the parlor, where Mrs. Kelly had gone to dust, then padded up the stairs. Quietly, I closed the door behind me as I stepped into the bedroom. I hardly ever came in here—it felt a little like trespassing.

Surveying my image in the mirror, I pinched my cheeks a few times. My face was rounder and fuller than it had been a couple of months ago—not quite so gaunt and sucked in—but my skin was still as drab as clay. I pinched until my cheeks had roses in them, wishing I could make myself healthy so simply. Then I sighed at the foolishness of the thought. I turned my back and again looked over my shoulder. This time, I could see clearly a big dark spot had spread along the very bottom of the seat. What in heck…?

There was nothing else to do but unbutton my overalls,

which was a pain. I lowered them down and turned and again looked over my shoulder. And then I froze.

Oh God.

Letting my pants fall to my ankles, I stared and stared, unbelieving. A big, bright red splotch had spread its way across the back of my drawers. Could I have cut myself somehow and not realized it? I knew I hadn't. It had to be coming from some-place…inside me.

Oh. I thought about the achy feeling I'd been having that morning. *Oh no.*

It was a wonder I managed to move. I felt my eyes rolling back a little, and then I got ahold of myself and tripped toward the bedroom door. I locked it, then stumbled backward a few feet, turning toward the Kellys' bathroom.

Behind the door I slowly pulled off my drawers, wincing. *Oh God*, it was true. There was blood all over my thighs. My very own blood everywhere! Of all the endings I had imagined for myself, I had never expected to go like this.

Frantically, I thought back over the Reverend's words the night I was cast out. He'd held up the Water of Judgment, saying something about my punishment, and then he'd told me what I would feel in the months before whatever ancient poisons it had in it finally killed me. Sleepiness, coughing, sickness, fever. He'd said I'd feel all of these things until my body finally broke down. Was this what he'd meant?

Teardrops fluttered on the ends of my eyelashes, blurring everything. I climbed into the bathtub, half naked, not wanting the blood to get on the Kellys' fine floor mat. Grabbing my ankles I brought my knees up to my face and closed my eyes. "I'm not ready," I whispered.

I'd been feeling better! The doctors...the Kellys...I'd thought I still had time.

The Kellys...

Just as the thought of them had come into my head, I heard the unmistakable sound of somebody jiggling the door in the bedroom.

"Glory?"

I sucked in my breath and held it. Somehow I hoped that if I didn't make a peep she'd go away.

"Glory? What's wrong?" Her voice was already high and crackly with worry, knowing me well, I figured. Well enough to worry about me being behind her locked bedroom door.

"Nothing," I called, singsongy as I could. Too singsongy. What could I tell her? Maybe I could just stay here and let the life drain out of me. Would it hurt too bad? Surely, with all this blood, the pain might become unbearable. If the Kellys took me to the hospital, they could give me some of that medicine that stops pain. But why hadn't the pain come already? Maybe I was too numb to feel it.

"Glory, dear, open the door."

I looked down at my legs again, then slapped a hand to my face with a new thought. It would be so embarrassing for Mrs. Kelly to know I was bleeding from...*down there.*

"Can you come back in a few minutes?" All I needed was time to think.

"Glory." This time, angry.

I took another deep breath and let it out.

"Coming." My voice came out hoarse and crackly. I got up and wrapped the nearest towel around my waist, then rubbed at my eyes with my right arm, trying to look less horrible than I felt, for Mrs. Kelly. I almost felt worse for her than I did for myself, for what I was about to tell her. I padded to the door. I turned the lock then stood back as she entered.

Before she could say anything, I blurted out, "I'm sorry."

She eyed me, worried and curious. "You're sorry for what, Glory?"

"I'm sorry for having to die on you, Mrs. Kelly. You've been so good to me. I don't want you to be sad about it."

"We've told you, Glory, you're not going to die," Mrs. Kelly said gently. "We're going to get you—"

"I am," I interrupted. "It's already happening. I'm bleeding."

Mrs. Kelly slapped her hands together and her eyes opened wide. "What?"

She searched my face, then looked down to the towel covering my lower half. Her eyes darted to the pile of overalls lying just off to my left, at the threshold of the bathroom. Then she looked back at my towel, then at me.

"From where are you bleeding?" she asked. I couldn't judge the look in her eyes. It was almost like relief, but also disbelief.

I looked at my feet. "Um, from my lower half."

"And it just started today?" she asked.

"Yes, ma'am."

"And you've never bled from your…lower half before?"

I squinted at her. "No."

What Mrs. Kelly did next left me speechless. Her face visibly relaxed into its usual soft, deep lines. She smiled, and then she bent over and gave me a hug. It was all I could do to keep hold of my towel.

She stood back and looked at me. "Honey, you're not dying," she said, her arms still around me, her voice soothing and calm. "You've gotten your period."

I stared at her, flabbergasted. My *period*?

"Yes." She grinned, giving me another squeeze. "Congratulations."

Yuck. Yuck yuck yuck.

I couldn't believe it. In fact, for a while I didn't.

Once, back home, before Theo and I got to the age when we only fought and teased each other, he told me he was taking me Wild Jeckyll hunting. I skipped along behind him, proud to be invited on the adventure, though I had no idea what a Wild Jeckyll was. Then, after about an hour of running me ragged, sending me to look behind this and that bush, Theo told me the truth. There was no such thing as a Wild Jeckyll—he'd made the whole thing up. Of course he laughed his head off while I ran home, fuming. I vowed to never, ever be so easily fooled again.

Maybe it was that old stubborn vow coming through, but Mrs. Kelly had a time convincing me that there was such a thing as a period. And even more of a time convincing me I wasn't dying— at least not now. The idea that every woman *had* a period, and that it all happened just like this—where you bled from *down there* while your belly ached in this strange, sharp way—was at first just too wild to be believed.

And then a thought hit me like a lightning bolt. "Are you

talking about the women's curse?" I asked, tilting my head to one side.

Mrs. Kelly shook her head, her thin lips clamping tightly together. "We're going to take you shopping," was all she said.

Back home, there'd been some mystery surrounding "becoming a woman." I remembered hushed conversations between Mama and my sister Teresa that would stop whenever the menfolk were around. They'd said, when I asked, that I'd understand when I was older. And a couple of times Mrs. White had told me I'd settle down when I "got the curse," filling me with dread and a fearful knowledge that the two were connected.

I'd vowed to her I'd never get it, making like I knew what it was. But I had never understood until, maybe, now.

Without my even asking, Mrs. Kelly was careful not to tell Mr. Kelly why we were going out—only that we were off to the drugstore and wouldn't be back for dinner. She'd dug up some kind of fluffy white pad from a box in my bathroom, and told me to wear it for the moment, until we got what we were after at the store. She seemed almost excited. She acted even nicer than usual.

It took me ten minutes in the bathroom (after I'd gotten new underwear and rinsed the other ones out in the sink) just to figure out how I was supposed to wear the darn thing. It took another five to leave the bathroom with any kind of dignity. In the car, my head was filled with dark thoughts. I was flaming with embarrassment. If this was what women had to deal with, it was a cruel joke. As if we weren't unlucky enough. Back home, women like Mama and my sister and me were supposed to do all the cleaning and cooking and boring stuff, and yet the men were supposedly in charge. In church, we got blamed for life's hardships because in the Bible Eve had gotten Adam to commit the first sin, and the Reverend was all the time calling women "wayward" and "Adam's downfall." It was so unfair.

But modern folks aren't like that. At least, not the ones I'd met. Dogwood, from what I'd seen since I'd been cast out, was a special case, with rules that didn't go along with everybody else's. I suppose that's why the town had broken off from the rest of the world in the first place, and why it was kept so closed up and separate. Most folks in the modern world didn't seem to go for things like "an eye for an eye" (like the Water of Judgment) or for women only wearing dresses and never getting a say in town affairs.

I thought of Becky, with her store and her Bob Dylan music, in charge of her own life even though she was married. And

Joe's mama—boss for a whole bunch of people. And Joe. He had never treated me as anything less than a person who had as many ideas and smarts as he did. I scowled deeper at the thought of him, and how unfair it was that I no longer had him as my friend. What would *he* think if he knew about my period? Did he know all women got them?

Luckily, once we were at the store, Mrs. Kelly took charge of finding what I needed. She grabbed a big pink shiny pouch and a smaller blue box from a high shelf. In fact, there was a whole wall filled with boxes the color of the rainbow, all seeming to be for the same purpose. I trailed behind her through the store, staring at the women around me. They all got their periods! I couldn't believe it. I thought about girls at school—ones I liked, like Joe's friend Sadie, and ones I didn't, like Stacy James. Did they get their periods, too?

"I have some aspirin in my purse, for the cramps," Mrs. Kelly said. "And a warm bath should help."

"A bath would be nice." I sighed as we left the store.

"But first," Mrs. Kelly said, draping an arm over my shoulder, "we've got to celebrate. Don't you think?"

She looked at me with such an excited, open expression that I didn't have the heart to tell her I'd rather pull my own toenails out than celebrate such an awful day. "Yes, ma'am," I said, smiling back.

Delmont Ave., as Mrs. Kelly called it, was lined with restaurant after restaurant—each lit up and glowing like a firefly in the dusk. Despite myself, I admired the prettiness of the electric lights. The night was warm and breezy, and several of the places had their glass doors pushed all the way open so that the inside was also the outside, open to the air. I could see people at many of the tables, eating. We pulled to a stop.

"Two please," Mrs. Kelly said as we stepped up to a small blond woman standing just inside of a place called the Sweetwater Café. At the same time, a smell filled my nostrils that was pure heaven.

"Right this way," the woman said, fetching up two menus from a shelf beside her and leading us across the room. Mrs. Kelly sailed along behind her while I gazed at the tables we passed. Some were empty, but most held two or more people along with plates of steaming, colorful food. Now, *this* was a true restaurant, like Katie and I had wanted to go to someday. The one I'd gone to with Joe—someplace called Denny's—had been such a disappointment. I'd felt bad afterward, like I hadn't really kept the promise to Katie to eat in a nice restaurant in Boston for her.

As we were seated, I stopped my gawking about and looked down at my fingernails, thinking of how it should have been Katie sitting here with me.

"It's not so bad, Glory," Mrs. Kelly said, leaning over the table to catch my eyes. I thought for a moment she understood, then realized she couldn't have. I'd never yet told her about Katie, though I'd told her most everything else. She was talking about the *period*. I pushed my memories out of my mind as she continued.

"It doesn't have to be. I know, you think it's the most embarrassing thing in the world. But the truth is, it's not. Not at all. I mean"—her eyes darted skyward and she shrugged—"it can be awkward sometimes, and uncomfortable, don't get me wrong. But it's also a gift. A blessing."

I stared, bristling inside. "Well, that is the biggest bunch of hooey I ever heard. I don't see what's so miraculous about"— the surprise on Mrs. Kelly's face made me swallow the end of my sentence—"it. Ma'am." I cleared my throat.

Mrs. Kelly sat back in surprise. She shrugged helplessly, like there was nothing she could say. And then she seemed to think better of it and spoke. "Well, certainly it doesn't feel like a blessing. Until you have a baby. *Then* you'll know. Then you'll be happy you have your period."

"*Pardon* me?" I squinted at her, not ornery, just confused. I didn't have the faintest idea what all this had to do with babies.

Mrs. Kelly got the same amazed, pitying look she'd had in the bedroom earlier. "For when you have a baby. You need to get your period to have a baby. Don't you…" I guess the look on my face told her all she needed to know. Her shoulders fell. "No. I don't suppose you do.

"Glory, your period is nature's way of making it so you can have babies. Didn't anyone ever tell you?"

"I'm gonna have a baby?" I whispered, clutching the edges of the table. But if I had a baby growing inside, what would happen to it if I died?

Mrs. Kelly shook her head violently, her expression halfway between laughing and crying. "No. No no no. You're not going to have a baby. It doesn't mean you're going to have a baby *now*. It means it's possible to have a baby *someday*."

I gazed at her, not disbelieving (what did I know about having babies anyway?), but boggled. "But. But everybody calls it…some folks call it a curse, don't they? Don't they want babies?"

Mrs. Kelly's eyes hardened. "It's nonsense. Glory"—she paused, waving her hand in frustration, searching for the right words—"nobody should make you feel ashamed or scared about something like this. 'Curse.' That's ridiculous."

"Well, it's just a different way of looking at it, that's all," I snapped. Her words were so sharp and confident and rueful that they burned me up, though I knew she was right. So folks back home had some things backward. Still, I didn't want anybody calling my family ridiculous.

"I'm sorry." Mrs. Kelly softened, putting her hand over mine and patting it. "Maybe *ridiculous* is too strong a word. I just…" She shook her head slightly. "I just wish the people who brought you up, whoever they might be, had done better by you. Maybe if you told me more about them, I'd understand."

Her eyebrows rose bravely. It usually went without saying that we did not talk about this. I guess the Kellys probably had an inkling of the kind of place I'd lived in growing up, what with my telling them about the Water of Judgment and such—things that set our town apart, or so I'd gathered, from the rest of the world. But I never talked about it much beyond that, for fear that the Kellys, or foster care, or the police would figure out exactly where it was, and take it into their heads to try to send me back.

I felt bad for snapping. If periods helped you have babies, the whole "curse" thing was kind of ridiculous. Babies are the most wonderful things in the world. I fought off thoughts of baby Marie, with her rosy cheeks and her sweet baby smell, and how I'd love to squeeze her so hard she'd melt.

"I guess." I cleared my throat. "I guess I see what you're saying. Only, well. Oh gosh." I sighed. "It's all pointless anyway."

"And why is that?" She tilted her head curiously.

Because I won't ever be a mama, I thought. But I knew it would upset her. And besides, we were going to see Dr. Filkin in a couple of days. Maybe she'd have some different, better news. "To think about stuff that's past," I said. "I'm saying, I believe you. I believe it's not a curse."

"Good." Mrs. Kelly picked up the menu. "Now, what'll we eat?"

The food was the very best I had ever had. Not wanting to ask any more ignorant questions that night, and not knowing what most of the names on the menu meant, I'd ordered the prettiest sounding item. Either it turned out to be a lucky guess, or else everything here was delicious. Every time I finished my glass of mint iced tea, Mrs. Kelly asked the waitress to bring me another. And then there was dessert: something called

Chocolate Puddles, which turned out to be two tiny, spongy chocolate cakes as soft as pillows, nestled on either side of a scoop of vanilla ice cream.

We talked the whole time, which was funny because in the Kelly home, there wasn't usually all that much conversation. The Kellys were quiet folks, friendly but very calm and relaxed. Still, something about being across a table from each other at a restaurant, and having the period topic to peck at, kept my foster mother and me there for more than three hours. A couple of times Mrs. Kelly referred to things that would either make me go crimson with embarrassment or snort iced tea up my nose and laugh.

In any case, by the time we walked out, I felt much better about the messy strange thing that was happening to my body. I even felt like…well, a woman, almost. That's what Mrs. Kelly kept saying I was. I almost wanted to write home and tell Mama and Daddy. Believe it or not, I almost even wanted to tell Joe.

Before going to bed that night—after we were home and I'd taken a nice, long bath—I walked into the kitchen to grab an apple. Mr. Kelly was sitting at the table, reading. I wondered if he knew about all that had been going on today. If he did, what did he think? I brushed past him and picked up the fruit, then padded back quietly, feeling my face grow warm. I didn't want to look him in the eye, not with the period business on my mind. But just as I passed the table again, he cleared his throat.

"Good night, Glory," he said.

I looked at him long enough to see that he was blushing. He fiddled with the pages of his book, sliding them between his fingers, avoiding my stare. He knew.

"Good night, Mr. Kelly."

He cleared his throat again. I shuffled my feet against the kitchen floor a couple of times. Then I patted his shoulder. "See you in the morning."

He shrugged, and smiled. "Not if I see you first."

Heading upstairs, I felt my whole face get even hotter. But I also felt touched that he would go through the trouble of getting embarrassed, just to say good night to little old me.

CHAPTER TWO

"Hello?"

"Hello, Mrs. Trew. It's Glory Mason. May I speak to Joe, please?"

I always used my best manners when I called the Trew house, even though I suppose I didn't have to use my last name anymore. After all, I spoke to Mrs. Trew all the time. And she always replied in this way. First she would sigh. And then she'd say, very kindly, "Hi, Glory. Let me go see."

She laid the phone down with a tap, and I heard her muffled footsteps retreat. My heart beat hard in my chest. Then the footsteps sounded again.

"Glory?"

It was still Mrs. Trew. *Darn. Darn darn.* "He can't come to the phone. Can I give him a message?"

I stared at my feet on the kitchen floor, fighting the lump in my throat. "Um, same message as last time, ma'am. Can you just ask him to give me a telephone call?"

"Yes, Glory, I'll do that." By the tone of her voice, I could tell I wasn't the only one who knew he wouldn't.

"Okay, bye." I laid the speaking part of the phone back on the hook, and kicked a toe at the linoleum floor with a squeak. It was so unfair. I'd finally gotten good at using the telephone, but the only person I knew to call didn't want to talk to me anymore. Wasn't that just like life? Everything that was supposed to be good always turned out rotten.

"Are you ready to go, Glory?"

Mrs. Kelly appeared in the kitchen with her usual sweet expression, and it made my scowl feel that much heavier on my face. Why couldn't I be more like her, always looking on the bright side of things? Sometimes I just wanted to break everything in sight.

"Who were you talking to?" Mrs. Kelly asked, eyeing my face closely all of a sudden.

"Nobody."

"Oh?" The look on her face hurt my conscience.

"Well, I just tried to call Joe, ma'am. But he wasn't there."

"Mmm." She nodded and kept eyeing me, then turned her attention to her purse. "That reminds me—Sherry called this morning. She wanted to know if she could come this Friday rather than next. I told her that would be fine."

"Why?" I asked. Child-welfare caseworkers were always supposed to see you on a schedule—as Sherry herself had explained to me once. I had to wonder why she'd come early.

Was it just me, or did Mrs. Kelly look uncomfortable? She shuffled through the slips of paper and clutter in her purse. "I'm... not sure." I waited for more. "Well, let's get going," she said. "We don't want to be late."

I nodded, shaking off my feeling of misgiving about Sherry. We were going to the doctor's office today, and they never liked it when you were late. We had already been late twice because Mrs. Kelly had had to scurry me out the door.

It wasn't that I hated going to the doctor so much as I hated thinking about going. I hated hoping they'd have great news (*Glory! We found out how to cure you! You're going to be fine!*) and being disappointed. They always shook their heads and told me they had to do more tests, and each time I felt so frustrated I could spit. But now, back in the car again, the same old hope curled around me and kept me silent and nervous.

"We haven't seen Joe in a while," Mrs. Kelly said after a moment.

"Yeah." I knew she wanted more, but I didn't want to talk about it. I didn't want to talk about *any* of the upsetting things in life—I just wanted to forget them. But then, it was all so hard to forget. It was hard, whenever I heard Joe's name, not to think of those spiteful things I'd said to him the last time we talked.

"Well, I've had a lot of friends over the years," Mrs. Kelly said, her eyes trained on the road ahead, "and some of them I thought would be around forever, but they weren't." She smiled. "On the other hand, with some I thought, 'This is it. It's over,' and they are still with me to this day. It's hard to tell, dear. Just don't let it make you afraid to keep trying." She leaned over and patted my leg.

I shrunk at Mrs. Kelly guessing so much about Joe and me, though I suppose it was all kind of obvious. But I wanted to take her advice to heart. With all the people I'd lost and couldn't have back, it made no sense to let Joe push me away. I just had to make him see how sorry I was. I *needed* to.

It gave me an ache in my heart to think on, especially when I remembered that day…before I'd ended up in the hospital, before all the horrible stuff that led up to it, there'd been the moment when we were walking…and he'd almost, almost held my hand. Hadn't he? I knew it was foolish, but that still kept me up at night sometimes, wondering. Had it been an accident or had he meant to do it? I remembered the feel of his fingers on my wrist and went all smushy and strange inside. Like being embarrassed, but in a good way. *But if he liked you that way then,* I told myself, *he'll never like you like that now.*

Still, Mrs. Kelly was right. I would keep trying. What did I have to lose?

Dr. Filkin's office was in a long, clay-colored building with a lot of other offices. Right next door was one with a big glowing foot in the window and a sign that said WE CARE ABOUT YOUR FEET! which made me ponder every time I came. How could anybody possibly care about feet? And what could a doctor do for your feet anyhow? I supposed they could take care of corns, but all you had to do with those was pry them out of your foot with a sharp knife. Maybe they could do something that was less painful, I supposed. And then give you fancy medicine to keep it from festering.

"Glory?" I looked up to see Mrs. Kelly waiting in the doorway, keeping the door open with one hand and waving me on with the other.

It always bothered me how bright it was in Dr. Filkin's office, and how many folks were waiting. The lights were so white and glary you felt like you were sitting on the moon, and the folks always made me antsy. For each one of them, the nurse would come out and call a name that wasn't mine, and

I'd nearly pee in my pants thinking it was my turn.

After we'd been sitting awhile the lady at the desk who kept track of things called my name. Another lady weighed me and poked at me a little, then ushered us into a small white room. I sat on the examining table swinging my legs while Mrs. Kelly perched nicely on a chair. We waited for what seemed like an hour until the creaking door finally announced Dr. Filkin's arrival.

This was our fifth time meeting, but I still felt as shy as could be around the doctor, and also flattered to be important enough to take up her time. First off, she was a woman doctor, which was unheard of back in Dogwood—and seemed even more amazing than being a woman boss like Joe's mama. And then, she was so smart. Her questions always came in quick, tight little sentences, one after the other, sharp as tacks—she never seemed to just ponder things but to jump right on them. If anybody could cure me, she would. To me, Dr. Filkin was like a magician. Or like what I used to think God was—somebody who looked out for you and could do anything.

"How are you feeling today, Glory, on a scale of one to ten?" She had her pen and paper poised for my answer.

"Um. I got my period." Then I put my hand to my mouth. I could not believe I had said that. But Mrs. Kelly had insisted it was a good sign, a *healthy* thing to have happened. So I supposed it was something the doctor would want to know.

"That's good," Dr. Filkin said, seeing my embarrassment but taking hardly any note of it. "Sometimes undernourished girls don't, and it's a bad sign when that happens—but you've been eating well and taking care of yourself, like we talked about, right?"

"Yes, ma'am." Mrs. Kelly had me eating three square meals a day and two snacks, and even though sometimes I couldn't eat it *all*, the scale the nurse had put me on said I'd gained weight.

"Does that include exercise?"

I looked at my feet. I knew about exercise, but I couldn't picture myself doing it. Back home, farmwork had been our exercise.

"Her school has a pool that's open in the summer," Mrs. Kelly jumped in, looking guilty. "I'm going to start taking her."

Dr. Filkin nodded, satisfied. "So you'd rate how you're feeling at…?"

"Um, an eight?" I said, sheepish. Aside from some cramps, which Mrs. Kelly had explained was part of the whole period thing, I felt pretty good. For a dying girl, anyway.

"Good. You haven't had any more of those…attacks recently

have you—any more fainting, vomiting…?"

"No, ma'am."

"Okay." She put down her notebook, lifted her shiny heart-listening tool (she'd mentioned what it was called, but it was too strange a word and I'd forgot) and put the black part up under her chin and into her ears. Then she felt all around my back and the top of my chest, making me take deep breaths. After that, she did the other usual stuff—checking my eyes and ears with a pointy flashlight, making me stick out my tongue.

I'd gotten used to this, since starting with Dr. Filkin. She had taken a "special interest" in my case, on account of there being obviously something wrong with me, bad enough to put me in the hospital, but something nobody had "put their finger on yet." And my admission about the poison, I suppose, that had gotten her attention. When I'd told her, she'd stopped in the middle of writing in her pad and just stared at me solemnly, nodding up and down. Then she'd gone off to talk with the Kellys alone. Since then, she'd gotten less serious and solemn, but she still kept an eagle eye on me.

Finally Dr. Filkin finished studying me and sat down. "Well, you look good, Glory." She sighed and put her hands together, leaning forward on her knees. "I have to tell you, our tests have all come back negative, which is a good and a bad sign. If you didn't keep having these episodes, I'd say you just had some kind of fatigue or virus.

"But of course there's a pattern here—your illness comes and goes. If it were a virus, we would most likely be able to spot it. And so if our tests are coming up negative, it means we haven't figured out how to fix anything."

I nodded, my heart sinking. She'd order more tests. There'd be more visits. More disappointment, probably.

"But of course I have my theories. Now, we've talked a lot about what you call the Water of Judgment, and that it was a punishment. I know you're in foster care. It seems you've been through quite a lot of trauma. I mean to say, things have been very emotionally difficult for you."

Dr. Filkin picked up her notebook again and scribbled on it, then ripped off the top page and handed it to me. I took it, and read another doctor's name.

"There's not much more I can do for you, at least for the moment. But I'd like to strongly suggest that you go see this doctor."

Another doctor? I could feel my eyes filling up with tears, and I looked up at the ceiling to keep them back. *Not much more I can do...*

"She's a psychiatrist," Dr. Filkin continued, cutting into my thoughts. *A what?* "You may not realize this, but the things that go on in your head can have a severe effect on your body. Dr. Keller can help you with the head part. I think it would do you a lot of good."

"What she means is," jumped in Mrs. Kelly, who could see how confused I was, "it's a doctor you can go and talk to. About the things that have happened to you. Somebody who wouldn't tell another living soul."

I stared back and forth at each of them, lost. "And that will help me with the poison?"

Now Mrs. Kelly and the doctor looked at each other somberly. I could tell what they were thinking was, *We don't know.*

"It's just that you've been through the mill, according to what you've told us. And it might help to have someone help you through it."

I still didn't understand, but I could feel my old stubborn streak silently roaring up inside. A doctor to help me go over all the rotten things that had happened since the night Katie and I broke into the shed and drank a bottle of wine for fun? Somebody to talk to about getting sent off from my family, not to mention letting my best friend drown in a cold, stupid lake? Maybe, maybe, if I had sixty years ahead of me it would be worth it to sit down with someone and tell them my story and talk and talk until it was all out of me, but that person sure as heck wouldn't be a *doctor*. And I sure as heck wasn't living another sixty years. Sixty *days*, maybe. What would be the point of dredging up all that pain, for someone like me? It would mean spending my last days in misery instead of the kind of peace I was trying so hard to keep. And they knew I was dying, didn't they? So why didn't they think of that, too?

I didn't say any of this, though. I just bit my lip, put the paper in my pocket, and managed a "thank you, ma'am" that sounded like it came from another girl. Not the Glory who used to speak her mind, or the Glory who believed in herself once, or even a Glory who was worth anything at all. This girl was still breathing, even smiling sometimes, but dead inside. She would have said "yes, ma'am" if Dr. Filkin had told her to sail away and become the queen of Spain, just to be polite.

On our way out, I was sure Dr. Filkin had given up on me, and let me down, and I would never see her again. I wondered if this was what Sherry was coming to see me about. Maybe she'd already heard—she was always checking in with the doctors on my case. Maybe they'd take me out of the Kellys' house, on account of me being a lost cause. "And remember the exercise," Dr. Filkin said to my back as we walked out the door. As if it would make any difference.

"Hey, look at that!" I shouted. I'd been wallowing in my own black thoughts, but now I shot straight up in my seat.

"What?"

Mrs. Kelly held the steering wheel steady as she craned to see the—well, what in heck was it? There were a few people milling about in and around it, or not so much milling as strolling. Some of them were stopped and bent over skinny silver poles—playing some sort of game, I gathered. But that wasn't what caught my eye.

There, arching between one group of people and another, was a tiny bridge—so small that I could have lain lengthwise across it and touched both ends. Below it was a clear flowing stream, and just beyond a windmill like the kind I'd seen in a book at school. There was even what looked like a tiny cliff, which poured into the stream like water from a pitcher. And all along the ground there was green—emerald green, like a carpet, or the shortest grass in the world.

"What *is* that place?" I sighed, enthralled.

"Oh, that? That's miniature golf. You didn't have that where you used to live?"

"No, ma'am," I admitted.

"Oh my, I used to love miniature golf. Back before we were

married, Jim and I played it at the boardwalk on our dates."

My breath quickened. "Can we play?" I turned pleading eyes on Mrs. Kelly, feeling bold. With the Kellys, I still hated asking for things—though I hadn't found it nearly so hard with the Aidens, who I'd been with for much less time. But I just had to get a try at miniature golf! It looked so enticing, like a tiny world. It reminded me a little of the palaces Katie and I used to build in the back of the granary back home. We'd used old boxes for shelves and hung gunnysacks to make a doorway, and most of the leftover space we called "the ballroom." When we were packed inside, so close and tight, we'd felt like mistresses of our own tiny kingdom. Only this looked so much closer to what we'd imagined.

But Mrs. Kelly shrugged apologetically. "What? Now? Oh nooo. I'm too old for that stuff now. And it's so muggy today."

"But please? Just once? We don't have to stay long." I knew I shouldn't beg, but I was just itching to see that little windmill, and the waterfall… What if I never had another chance?

"Maybe you can get a friend to go with you. Some other day." Mrs. Kelly didn't seem to notice my desperation. She hummed a little tune to herself under her breath.

I felt like all the wind had come out of me. Mournfully, I watched through my window as the miniature golf place disappeared behind us. It was so unfair. I felt convinced I'd never get to go there, now.

Had I really made a mistake, coming here and living with the Kellys? I couldn't shake the bitter feeling inside that I'd landed in the wrong spot. That if I had younger foster parents, or if I'd just stayed back with Becky Aiden and her funny, rambunctious kids, I'd be living out my last days a little more fully. How was I supposed to see the world, when I lived with folks who had already seen it all?

I stole a glance at Mrs. Kelly's sweet face, etched by all the things she'd experienced herself. *Glory, you are being unfair. Just forget it.* I sighed, opening the part inside me where all the disappointments went, and dumping this in. It was another thing I'd lock away where it wouldn't bother me.

It was another thing I couldn't do anything about.

CHAPTER
THREE

"I'll see you at four."

"Okay, bye, Mr. Kelly. Thank you."

"You remember the number, right, in case you need us?"

"Yes, Mr. Kelly."

"And you have the twenty dollars I gave you?"

"Yes, sir."

I balled up my hand in front of my lips to hide a pleased smile. Mr. Kelly was so goofy sometimes. Ever since the hospital, he'd been my good buddy, sometimes falling over himself to make sure I was all right. Often at dinner, he'd lean over his plate in the silence, give me a look from under his bushy eyebrows, and ask, "How *are* you, Glory?" Once, though, he'd said, "Hey, good-lookin', whatcha got cookin'?" instead, surprising me so much that I nearly choked on my meat loaf. Coming from a man who I'd first thought was so quiet and gruff, his concern and his goofy jokes always gave me a warm, tickled feeling.

Now he scowled back at my amused expression, but only jokingly. "Okay, okay," he said. "See you at four."

I slammed the door and watched him drive off, then turned toward the school.

What a relief it was to be here and not be *going* to school. But I also ached a little, wishing it were September, and time to go back. I would have liked to see a few of my teachers again, especially Mrs. Blackburn. And of course Joe wouldn't be able to avoid me completely if we ended up sharing a class or two. It would be nice just to see his face.

I didn't know if it was the helpless mood Dr. Filkin had put me in, now that she'd given up on me, but I shivered. *I won't make it back to school*, I thought. *I won't see September.*

Oh, Glory Mason, don't be a ninny. I strode toward the school building, full of purpose. *A year.* I was supposed to have a year. That gave me till January, and I felt fine. But as I walked I tried to picture being back at school, or seeing the leaves turn again, or dressing in my warm fall clothes—and the picture wouldn't come.

I sighed, reaching the double doors to the rec hall. I'd *keep* myself well. I'd eat well, and think peaceful thoughts, and exercise, too, starting now. I pushed open the doors.

Whoa.

The rec hall was a big building connected to the school gym. I'd always wondered about it, but had never actually gone in. Now I saw that it was much roomier inside than I'd even figured on, with a sprawling, gray tile floor. The pool itself was a rectangle, a shock of blue in the middle of all the gray.

What made me stop in my tracks was all the kids. There must have been about twenty of them—all gathered in knots in and around the water. Their voices echoed loudly off the tiles, jarring my brain and making me uneasy. Mentally, I contrasted the scene to the lake back home where we used to swim. It had been still and quiet, nestled in the woods, full of fish and toads and sided by a couple of giant oaks, surrounded by dense underbrush. Peaceful. Like so much of what I'd left behind, it had been better.

Then again, in the winter, when it had been covered in ice, the lake had cracked open and swallowed Katie, giving her back to me half-dead and when there was already nothing anyone could do. If I really thought about it (I decided not to) I should be grateful it didn't remind me more of that place.

I clutched my swim bag and stepped forward, looking for a spot where I could put it down. Shyness made my heart beat quicker. All these strange faces. There were even a few familiar ones—from school, which somehow made it worse. Should I say hello to them? For the millionth time since I'd left home, I felt out of place. Thank goodness my period was over, for now. I would have felt even more self-conscious.

Wheeeeeeeeeet!

Ouch. I scanned the room to see where the awful noise had come from, and spotted a man sitting on the one chair by the side of the pool, a silver whistle in his mouth. A sign on the arm of his chair read LIFEGUARD.

He was awfully eye-catching—tanned and muscular and strong looking. I studied him, partly for his handsomeness, and also just thinking how nice it was, him watching all these kids. That was clearly what he was doing—he kept making hand gestures to let people know when they were being too rough. And all the while he talked with some of the kids, one boy in particular, who seemed to be asking him something.

As I watched he leaned forward to allow the boy to hear him better, and then my heart skipped a beat. Just beyond him, in a maroon two-piece bathing suit that showed her pretty curves, was Sadie, one of the few people I'd been friendly with at school. And to her left, involving himself in the conversation with the lifeguard, was none other than Joe. *My* Joe.

He had one hand resting on his hip, just above his baggy blue swim shorts, and the water was dripping down his arms and chest, and down from his hair onto his face. As he talked, his free hand waved around for emphasis, and his brown eyes went from one person to the other. I knew I should move, or at least look away. But I stood still as a stone, only roiling and mixed up on the inside.

I guess Sadie saw me first. She waved, catching my eye and Joe's attention. He followed her gaze. For a second he seemed to meet my eyes, but then he stared off to my right. In another moment he was back in his conversation.

Had he seen me? Sadie was waving me over now. I searched my mind for some way to ignore her without being rude. But I had to admit, I was stuck.

I held up a finger to say "wait a minute," then I slid off my shirt and T-shirt and laid them on top of my bag. I hoped I looked okay in this bathing suit. It was deep red and my skin was terribly pale next to it. Like milk and cranberries. *Well, no matter.* I smoothed my brown hair back behind my shoulders as I padded across the tiles.

Sadie had grasped Joe's arm, and now she pulled him along to meet me halfway, a few feet from the edge of the pool. I swallowed the jealousy her easiness with him made me feel. *I shouldn't care*, I thought, lifting my chin. In fact, I hoped they liked each other. *That* way. If they did, good for them.

"Hey, stranger!" Sadie said, giving me a little push on the arm. "Where have you been?"

I forced the two corners of my mouth upward in a wooden smile, my eyes directly on Sadie's. I was too nervous to even *look* at Joe. "Oh, I've just been...*hanging out*." Gosh. How fake did that sound? I didn't half know what *hanging out* really meant, let alone actually do it. "How is your summer...going?" I stared at Sadie so intently as she answered, my eyes felt like they were crossing.

"Great." She looked over my shoulder. "You know you can change in the locker room, right?"

I followed her gaze to my lump of clothes, which appeared to be the only lump of clothes in the room. I felt too dumb to reply.

"How 'bout you, how's your summer?" she asked brightly, when I didn't answer. I searched for something to tell her, thinking I might try to include Joe somehow with a glance or a smile. But just as I began, he moved and caught my eye. He was turning away, and in another moment he was walking off toward the pool, just like that. Snubbing me. Sadie and I both stared after him. My fingers tapped on my thighs tensely, and inside, my heart creaked and groaned like an old floorboard.

Sadie's expression was surprised as she turned to me, but

also apologetic. I hated how sorry she seemed, and I hated looking so foolish and hurt. This left no doubt in my mind, if there had been any before. He wanted nothing to do with me.

"He's a stubborn one," she said. Then she leaned in and lowered her voice. "He still hasn't told me what you guys are fighting about."

"We're not...well...it's my faul—"

"Well, he should get over it," she interrupted airily. "Anyway, you've called. You've tried."

Her words hit me like knives. He had told her about it—poor Glory calling him and wanting to make up! Or, more likely, she'd been there, at his house, when I'd tried. He'd been "available" for her, but not for me. "I called a couple of times," I said, trying to sound equally airy, my pride wounded on top of everything else.

But Sadie wasn't fooled. She took my hand. "Don't worry about him. He'll get over it. C'mon," she nudged. "You're coming in." With that, she smiled warmly and tugged me toward the pool, as if this were just a small problem I could forget.

She kept hold of my hand as we approached the water's edge. "Jump in on the count of three," she said. I nodded solemnly. I'd always been a good swimmer. Theo had taught me the hard way—tossing me into the lake a few times and making me kick for it. But now I wasn't in the mood.

"One, two, three." Hands clasped, we leaped off the side, into the water. The voices of the other people became hollow and muffled. I opened my eyes, holding my nose, and watched all the bubbles we'd made go up, up, and up.

"Who is President Eisenhower?"

"What is Beech?"

"What are the Dardanelles?"

Mrs. Kelly alternately balled her fists or bit her lip as she blurted out the answers for our nightly game of *Jeopardy!* Of all the times I'd seen her watch it, and the times I'd played with her, the show had never failed to excite her. She didn't get that way about anything else. Even now, she was calm and dignified, just a little less than usual.

"What is a fleet fleet?" I managed to yell, winning my first points of the night.

"Good job, dear," she said, glancing at me for a brief moment, then turning back to the television. We didn't compete against each other like the contestants. We were a team.

We'd been playing together for two weeks, but it had quickly come to feel like a tradition. After dinner, Mr. Kelly would leave his spot by the TV empty so his wife and I could hunker down and get ready for the program to start. Then we'd make comments about the contestants while they were introduced. (Me: "Look at those eyebrows." Mrs. Kelly: "Isn't she a tiny little thing?") Finally the clues would start coming. Most of the time, either Mrs. Kelly knew the answer or neither of us did. But once in a while, when there was a Bible category, or something having to do with word puzzles like fleet fleet (the clue was "fast ships") I got a point or two in.

"Thanks." I sighed. Well, it was no miniature golf, but at least I felt like I was learning something.

"Oh," Mrs. Kelly said as soon as the first batch of commercials had started. "I forgot. You got a letter today. I put it on your bed."

My heart skipped. "A letter?"

"Yes." Mrs. Kelly nodded. "Up on your bed."

Bewildered, I stood up without another word and padded into the hall, then on up the stairs. Who in the world could have sent me a letter?

Right away, I knew who I *hoped*. It made the air leave me, so that I was panting when I reached the upstairs.

It had been weeks since I'd mailed my first and only postcard home. Could they have gotten it and replied? It was all I could do not to burst into a run. Could it really be from them? What would the letter say if it was? Would it be from Mama or Daddy? Would it give me a cure for the poison? An invitation to come home? Even if it was just words—just a few words about anything, I'd be over the moon.

I pushed the bedroom door open as slowly and nervously as if the devil himself had been standing behind it. There, in the middle of my pink room, lying on top of the pink bedspread, was the letter.

I took it between my fingertips, noticing it was covered in red-and-blue smudges. Looking closer, I could see they were stamps, with words like *Forward To* and *Mail Processing*. A bunch of words on the front had been crossed out, and written beside them was the Kellys' address. And then, in the upper left corner, where I knew return addresses were supposed to go, was the name. *Aiden. Mrs. Rebecca Aiden.*

I slumped down onto the mattress. Becky. Not Mama and Daddy, but Becky. *Dumb.* How would the folks back home know how to reach me anyway? I hadn't even *put* my return address on my postcard, I now remembered. I hung my head in my hands for a second, the envelope crinkling up against me, and took a deep breath. Then I rubbed my face and sat up straight again, staring down at the envelope.

It was a wonderful thing, I knew, to hear from Becky. When

I'd needed money, she'd given me a job at her store. When I'd needed to feel cared for, she'd been a friend—inviting me into her home, taking care of me like a mother would. It'd been my lucky day when she'd come into my life, and I was eager to hear how she was doing, not to mention thrilled she still liked me enough to write. But when I tore at the envelope and pulled the letter out, it was with a sinking feeling of loss.

Dear Glory,

First of all, I want you to know how rotten it was of you to make us worry so. When I found your letter the morning you left, I had a thousand images of you getting kidnapped or murdered on the high-way before I'd gotten halfway through the first sentence. We were all beside ourselves. It wasn't nice. But I'm not writing to scold you, sweetie, I just have to get it out of the way first! Now on to more pleasant things (I hope).

I'm so glad you found your way to Social Services, or that they found their way to you. I guess you may not have wanted that, but selfish as it may sound, what matters to me is that you're safe. I hear you are with foster parents. I hope they're treating you well. You deserve the best.

I don't understand fully why you left, but I've been assuming you had an inkling that Nick and I had already contacted someone about you, and told them that you might be a runaway. I know, it was a sneaky thing to do. Please understand that it was only because we— and I mean both me and Nick—were concerned about you. You're a kind, loving girl and I know you have your reasons for all the secrets you keep. I simply cannot believe you would have done any of this, including bailing on us, if you didn't feel you had to. Which is why I still trust you completely, despite everything (I hope you still trust me). And why I'm writing to tell you, we still want you to be a member of our family. I know Nick wasn't as welcoming as he could have been, but he's included in that we I promise. We all miss you. Amelia, in fact, is looking over my shoulder right now to make sure I say that clearly enough.

Glory, I've approached the center and begun filling out all the paperwork I'd need to adopt you. Now, before you feel like I'm taking over your life, let me say that this is completely your choice. If you are happy where you are, I am happy for you (though I'd rather you be here with us). But if you're not, or if you're not sure, please think about it. I'm going to keep working on the paperwork because apparently it takes a while, but I won't do anything solid until I hear a yes or no from you. Just please, think about it. Don't feel like you don't have a place here anymore—because you do.

Did you ever even know my number? It's 555-7076. And the shop, remember, is 555-0661. Send a letter if that's better for you, as soon as you decide. They said at the center you could make the move at any time once we're approved to be foster parents, and then from there we can work on adopting you officially. But again, Glory, this is all up to you. As far as I'm concerned, the sooner we have you back in our arms, the better.

Talk to you soon, I hope.

Much love, Becky

I didn't fold the letter right away, but held it against my chest, right where I ached. I held it there for a long while, staring at the window across from my bed. All I kept thinking was, *The Aidens still want me.* Over and over again. I'd known what I'd done—leaving in the dead of night—was rotten, though I *had* felt like I had to do it. I guess it wasn't that the Aidens had forgiven me that surprised me. I already knew they had big hearts. It was the wanting me and loving me, still. Even Mr. Aiden.

I put the letter down and went out into the hall, then into the bathroom. I turned on the light and closed and locked the door, then stared into the mirror. Same face as always, same brown eyes, same pale skin and straight features. Why would someone love me? I looked in my eyes and tried to figure it out. What was it about me that could be lovable to someone like

Becky, who didn't even *have* to love me, someone who wasn't kin? I honestly didn't know. I surely wasn't lovable to myself, not anymore. But I did still have pride, and manners. And I could still laugh sometimes, and talk clever every once in a while. Was that what it was?

I didn't think too much about Katie these days, except in that vague picture way. I didn't even think about home a lot, if I could help it. And I definitely tried not to think about all those things I didn't like about myself. But looking in the mirror, I was kind of hard to ignore. And it was like sinking into a pit, thinking of all the reasons I *shouldn't* be loved.

Finally I turned out the light and went back into my room. I wasn't sure what to do with the letter. What would the Kellys think if I showed it to them? What would they think of me being invited to go live with the Aidens? Would they be sad? But wasn't that what foster parents were supposed to do—keep you until you were adopted? I'd certainly wished more than once that I could be back with the Aidens, for so many reasons. It seemed impossible, though. What about me being sick? Could it actually happen, before I died? Could I spend my last weeks or months with the Aidens? The thought of it made my stomach ache.

I folded up the letter and put it neatly back into its envelope, then tucked it away in my special hiding spot in my bureau, with my family picture and Jake's letter. I resisted the urge to pick those things up and look at them. Doing it only ever brought me heartache.

Instead I went back downstairs and caught the last five minutes of *Jeopardy!* I didn't say a word about the letter. I didn't know where to start.

CHAPTER
FOUR

Tara Kelly's old room still felt like it was hers instead of mine. I'd taken a navy blue scarf the Kellys had bought me and draped it over the bureau. I'd pulled down the big pink curtains and taped a few pictures from magazines—of flowers, and foreign places, and houses I liked—on the walls. But the room was still the Kellys' daughter's, through and through, despite her being dead so long.

Sometimes I liked to curl up on the bed in the sun like a cat and read—I'd read books like *Little Women* and *The Catcher in the Rye*, which had lots of cusswords and would have shocked folks back home to no end—but I always thought of it as being in *her* spot. I often wondered if Tara had also liked to lie in the sun. She was half on my mind the next morning as I read Becky's letter again and again, my chin perched on my hands and the letter between my elbows on the bed. She and the Kellys.

The sooner we have you back in our arms the better. My eyes kept darting back to those words. How lovely to be Amelia Aiden's roommate again, up late talking and telling stories. I'd know better than to get annoyed at her chattering—this time, I'd appreciate it. It would be heavenly to sit around the dinner table with her and Bo and Andrew, making jokes. A *real* life, for however long it might last.

But could I really leave the Kellys? I thought of them sitting downstairs, so unsuspecting. I felt awful for not telling them about the letter already. But if I told them now, before I decided, they might try to convince me not to go. And I needed to make the decision for myself. I mean, these were the last months of my life at stake, and I wanted—no, *needed*—to do the right thing. *No more mistakes, Glory. This time you will do things right.*

"You ready to go?"

I slapped both hands over the letter. Mr. Kelly stood in the doorway, wearing a button-down plaid collared shirt, his car keys jingling from his hand. He looked like one of those kindly grandpas on a television show.

"Yes, sir," I said. "I'll be right down." I waited for him to go. He muttered to himself, then said out loud, "Dairy Queen."

"Sir?"

"You look like you're in the mood for Dairy Queen."

I tried to control a wry smile. I knew Mr. Kelly loved ice cream from Dairy Queen. I also knew he was using me as an excuse to go there. It had happened twice already. He'd take me and buy me a peanut butter parfait and then get a chocolate-covered cone for himself, saying this would be "just between us." Then we'd sit there and eat in comfortable silence, with him clearly relishing every bite. Mrs. Kelly didn't allow him to eat sugar.

"That sounds good, Mr. Kelly."

Satisfied, he simply nodded, then disappeared downstairs. With a sinking feeling, I picked up the letter again, folded it, and tucked it under my mattress.

We were going back to the pool again, and I didn't know which was worse: having to see Joe there and be miserable, or sitting here feeling guilty about the Kellys, and the new secret I was keeping. Luckily, I guess, I didn't have a choice.

I'd have to tell the Kellys sometime soon. But not right now.

He was the first person my eyes went to when I walked in through the double doors, a little later than usual thanks to my stop at Dairy Queen with Mr. Kelly. His back was to me, but Joe Trew had this tall, confident way of standing that made it easy to pick him out. I quickly looked away, then scanned the area around him to see if Sadie was there. She wasn't. I didn't know whether to be disappointed or relieved. At least it meant I could keep to myself.

I went to the locker room and changed, then made my way to the shallow end of the pool—completely opposite where Joe stood. Kids were splashing and yelling everywhere. I nibbled my lip. *Tomorrow, I'm telling the Kellys. No way am I coming here anymore.* But I also cursed myself. Why did I have to be so darn shy? And why, oh why, did Joe have to be here?

Without looking at anyone else, I walked into the water and dunked myself. I swam up to the wall and held on to the edge, facing away from all the activity. Then I held my nose and ducked underwater again, this time letting out all my breath.

My backside touched the bottom, and I put my hands against the ground. How long could I stay under? I wondered. A minute? Two minutes? An hour? That would show Joe, wouldn't it, if I held my breath longer than anyone else in the world ever had? I'd finally surface, and everyone would cheer. Then I thought of Katie, and came up for air.

"Hey!"

"Hey you!"

My hair was in my eyes. I flipped it back and turned around to see a gaggle of kids on the side of the pool, staring at me.

Instinctively, my arms crossed over my middle. Had I done something wrong?

Then I glanced around, and saw that I was the only one left in the pool.

"We want to play Sharks and Minnows," one of the girls said. "We're not allowed to do it if you're in there."

I felt my cheeks going red. I scanned the faces for Joe, wondering if this was his way of getting back at me—to trick me somehow. But he appeared to be busy talking to another boy, still not noticing me. The lifeguard shrugged at me, indifferently.

Well. I climbed on the ladder to my left and hoisted myself up. Everyone else scurried into a line alongside the pool, except for one tall, freckly boy who stood across from them and suddenly yelled, "All minnows into the water!"

Within a moment, everyone had jumped into the pool, sending up splashes everywhere. I watched as the freckly boy dove in after them, tagging one and then going after another. Finally, several people had reached the opposite wall and were climbing out again while the freckled boy swam over to my side and pulled himself onto the tiles. The ones he'd tagged followed him and seemed to join his team. And then the whole thing repeated itself, again and again. The number of minnows got smaller and the number of sharks got bigger, until there weren't any minnows left (Joe was one of the last ones to go, I noticed). And then the game started over.

I didn't know what to do. I felt dumb just watching but I also felt wary of joining in. Still, it looked like an easy enough game. I was a strong swimmer. And if Joe didn't like me playing (surely he'd seen me by now), well, I couldn't help that.

At the next turn, I lined up alongside everyone else.

"All minnows into the water!"

In a riot of splashes my fellow "minnows" disappeared. I stood on the wall, watching as the "shark" went after one, then another. My plan was to wait for the best possible time to jump. I wanted him to be completely distracted when I dove in so I could slip right past easily; I wondered why nobody else had thought of it. Then suddenly the shark was coming toward me. I stepped back from the edge.

"You gotta jump!" I heard somebody yell from the other side.

"Jump!" a few more repeated.

The boy was almost right under me now, and the other kids kept yelling, and I knew I had better jump though I wasn't quite sure why. Just as the boy was about to touch the wall, I took a running leap and sailed over his head. Then I was in the water and kicking with all my might. And then my hand came hard against the wall. Safe!

Elated, I pulled myself out by my arms and stood up next to all the other minnows who were still safe, ready to do the whole thing over again. We went through three more rounds, and I was one of the last people caught. I knew I could do even better.

My eyes kept drifting to Joe, though, as if he were a magnet, and I kept feeling bad when he got caught before me. The third time, I watched sorrowfully as he frowned and wrinkled up his forehead, frustrated, and lined up with the other people who'd been turned into sharks. I knew Joe was a good sport, but he also hated losing. He was proud. I, of all people, could understand that.

There were only three people on the minnows' side now, besides me. I stood up straighter—determined, this time, to be the last one caught.

"All minnows into the water!"

Diving right away, my heart racing again, I cut underwater to the right. I couldn't see much of what was ahead of me, but it looked like there were no sharks between me and the wall. To my left, I saw someone get tagged, but I was home free! The wall loomed up, and I reached out my hand, and...*ouch!* Something had grabbed me around one ankle. I shot up for air, spluttering, just short of safety. *Darn.* Whoever it was, their fingers were still digging into my skin. Annoyed, I turned, rubbing the hair away from my eyes.

And there was Joe, looking me straight in the eye for the first time all day—triumphant. He let go of my foot, stared at me another minute, as if I were a flea he wanted to squash. I was too startled to do or say a thing. And then before I could, he'd turned and raced off.

Joe got caught before me again after that, four times. Each time, as soon as he'd turned into a shark, he'd come after me and tag me. He didn't say a word, or smile like he was having fun. He just waited for me to see it was him who'd got me, and then took off.

At first, I just felt bewildered and sorry about it. But then, by the third time, it had gotten annoying. Try as I might, I couldn't escape him. I was a faster swimmer, I reckoned. But it was impossible to escape a shark when they had their sights set on you alone.

Finally I realized I had to get a new plan. If Joe wanted a

fight I'd give him one. The next round, I let myself get caught right away. Now the shoe was on the other foot! How would Joe like *me* being the shark?

"Gotcha!" I yelled. Again and again. Joe seemed to get madder and madder as I kept catching him, but he still didn't say one word to me. Soon we were both trying to get caught first so we could be sharks and get each other.

At one point, I couldn't even get caught—the shark was busy chasing after others. I tried to look like I was at least making a try for it, but finally I began to tread water and yelled "Hey, over here!" When I finally climbed out after being tagged, the freckly boy who'd started the game was staring at me. Joe happened to be just behind him.

"You guys are ruining the game," he said, his hands on his hips. "Can you just forget about flirting with each other and play?"

"What'd you say?" Joe said, resting his hands on his waist and leaning forward as if he couldn't have heard correctly, making the boy turn around to face him. Meanwhile I stared at the goose bumps popping out all over my arms, mortified. Boy, did he have it wrong.

But there was no time for them to argue. The next round began, and the boys, along with all the other kids, quit talking and leaped into the water. Shivering on the pool's edge, I made sure nobody was looking, and then padded off toward the locker room.

I felt scolded, and embarrassed, and stupid. Most of all I felt hurt, that this was where Joe and I had ended up—being nasty to each other. Mr. Kelly had given me change for the phone to keep in my swim bag, in addition to the twenty dollars. He wanted me to have it in case I needed him to come get me early.

I couldn't think of a better time to use it.

CHAPTER FIVE

"Hey, Glory!"

Sherry stood in the great white doorway of the Kelly home, a vision of summer in sunglasses and short pants. She looked so breezy and cheerful as she greeted me and Mrs. Kelly that I felt instantly relieved. She didn't act like a person who'd come on serious business as I'd feared.

After exchanging all sorts of niceties, we stepped out into the backyard, where Mr. Kelly was pouring tall glasses of iced tea. We sat at the white wrought-iron table, basking in the sun and a light breeze, talking about this and that.

"I hear you have a clean bill of health, Glory," Sherry said, leaning toward me but also glancing at Mr. and Mrs. Kelly for a moment. "The blood tests all came back negative?"

"That's right," Mrs. Kelly offered for me, smiling.

Sherry nodded like she truly believed it was good news. "You do look so much better. Your cheeks are pink."

I shrugged, flattered. I knew Sherry was right, I was looking better than I had. But wasn't it true that creatures often rallied before they died? Back home, I'd seen it happen with cattle. And, I remembered especially, one of the horses that had just given birth. Katie, so softhearted, had come to our door crying and telling us it had died, which had shocked all of us because it'd been up and around that afternoon. So maybe looking and feeling better wasn't such a good sign. After all, there wasn't any reason I might be getting better.

But I didn't have a mind to stop the flow of pleasant talk. It was nice to have someone around besides the Kellys, a new voice to listen to. And Sherry had always been kind to me. In fact, I could have sat there happily chatting all afternoon, but the Kellys seemed to have other ideas. As if on cue, after about half an hour, they both stood up and said they were going inside. "To let you have your privacy," Mrs. Kelly said.

When I turned back to Sherry after watching them disappear into the house, she was looking suddenly serious. *Oh no*. Had she heard something from the doctors that I hadn't? Something the Kellys couldn't tell me themselves?

"Glory, I do have a reason for coming today."

"Yes, ma'am," I replied, looking down at my fingernails.

"Have you received the letter from Rebecca Aiden?"

I gulped, surprised. And nodded.

"Well, she has been in touch with the center, and recently with me, specifically. About the possibility of adopting you." She eyed me a moment for my reaction, but then continued. "She and her husband have qualified to be foster parents; we approved them this past week." Still, I said nothing. "I know you have a"—she crossed her arms thoughtfully—"history with them.

"We try to take care of these things as quickly as possible, to minimize the trauma of transitions between one home and another. So I wanted to come over here and talk to you about it in person."

Sherry leaned forward on her elbows. "Glory, what do you think about going to live with them?"

What did I think? What *did* I think?

Sherry looked worried. "I see you're kind of shocked. You did get the letter, right?"

"No, ma'am."

"No?"

"No. I mean, I'm not shocked. I mean, I got the letter. I'm just confused."

Sherry put a hand on my shoulder. "That's fine. It's okay to be confused. It's a lot to absorb."

We sat in silence for a few moments while I tried to harness my thoughts. Sherry waited patiently. "I...I have *absorbed* it, I suppose. I...I really like Becky. I think I'd like to go back. But...how long would it all take?"

First things first. There was no point even considering it if I was gonna die before anything happened.

Sherry looked puzzled. "Not long. A move could happen immediately, actually, since they've already qualified as foster parents. Are you so eager to leave the Kellys?"

"No," I whispered, shaking my head passionately. My heart began to throb. "No. I l...ike the Kellys." I'd been about to say *love*. "I just, do you think they'd be okay if I left?"

Sherry smiled sympathetically. "Well, they already know it's a possibility. We've spoken about the situation and—"

You could have knocked me over with a feather. "You've talked about...me moving away?"

"Yes, and you know, they are your *foster* parents, Glory. They've always known this was a possibility."

Now a stinging was in my chest, and I couldn't put my finger on it. I felt so hurt all of a sudden.

"So the Kellys...they don't mind?"

"Well, I can't answer for them," Sherry said vaguely. "It's something you all need to discuss."

Discuss? I had the thought that I'd rather wear girlie dresses every day. It just didn't seem right, me and the Kellys sitting over spaghetti, talking about parting ways as if...as if we didn't mean anything to one another.

My stomach sank.

Gosh have mercy, Glory. I should have been relieved. I was the one thinking of leaving. It was lucky that the Kellys wouldn't mind.

Sherry was talking, and I quit my thoughts to listen. "...biological parents. Should they be located, they would have the right to sue for custody. Of course, at that point we'd need to investigate whether they were fit guardians or not." I figured out she was talking about my real mama and daddy. "And Glory"—she shifted in her seat—"if there's a reason you left, that you've been keeping... If they abused you, in any way, that would be a different story. You can still tell me. I need you to tell me, sometime. And you need it, too. It would be good for you."

Oh gosh. Here it was again. Why were modern folks so heck bent on talking and talking about things? Back home, when you went through something painful, you were supposed to keep a stiff upper lip. When it was physical pain, you bit down on a cloth while Doc stitched you up or whatnot. And that was pretty much the same way you dealt with things that hurt on the inside. Bite down. Talking about things was not for us.

But, I wondered, did poisoning a girl count as *abuse?* I supposed in the modern world it did. But I wasn't a modern girl, I was a Dogwood girl—way deep on the inside. And in Dogwood, the poison was just justice. Sherry would never understand that. Then again, she hadn't even brought up the Water of Judgment. Which seemed like something that should come up here, what with all the talk of moving on to a "new life." Was she really optimistic enough to think I was cured?

I stretched and fidgeted in my chair, my fingers and toes itching with frustration. We talked for a few more minutes, but I had a lot to weigh on my mind, and I guess Sherry could see that. She stood up to go inside.

In the kitchen, Mrs. Kelly was fixing dinner and Mr. Kelly was on the telephone. I could hardly look at them for all the hurt I felt, and the embarrassment for having things so wrong.

Mrs. Kelly put down the spatula she was holding and wiped her hands with a cloth. "Well, you two," she said, but didn't finish the sentence. It was like she was nervous, and couldn't think of something to say. I braced myself—it seemed like a big talk was coming. But it didn't happen.

"You're leaving so soon, Sherry?" she finally asked. "You know, there's a shortcut back to Beechtree from here that Jim always takes…" And that was how it went. It reminded me of when I'd first met Mrs. Kelly, the way she'd chattered on as we escorted Sherry into the hall.

At the front door, Mrs. Kelly fell silent, and Sherry turned to give me a meaningful look. "I'll call to check in a day or two," she said. "In the meantime, I know you'll be thinking things through."

I nodded uncomfortably, what with Mrs. Kelly right there listening, then said good-bye, closing the door behind her.

We three—Mrs. Kelly and I, and now Mr. Kelly who'd walked up behind us—stood in the foyer for a moment, silent. I could see from the looks on their faces that they felt sorry and anxious—maybe worrying about my feelings the same way I'd worried about theirs. I couldn't remember being this uncomfortable in their house since the day I'd moved in. Suddenly I felt like I didn't know them at all.

Fool Glory. I'd thought I had.

CHAPTER
SIX

Is it only me, or are things often different from what they seem?
Do other people get ideas stuck so deep in their heads that they
can't see the truth with their own two eyes? A person who feels
well can be sick. Memories you've pushed down deep can jump
out at you all of a sudden, without so much as a peep before-
hand.

The morning after Sherry came, I wandered downstairs to
breakfast, expecting the big talk the Kellys and I were sure to
have. I dreaded seeing the looks on their faces, strained and anxious like the night before. I'd resolved, sometime between last
night and this morning, to put their anxiety to rest, and tell them
it was okay—that I didn't mind if they wanted to let me go.

But to my surprise, when I entered the kitchen, Mr. Kelly
was bent over a crossword puzzle and didn't even seem to
notice I'd entered the room. Mrs. Kelly held a skillet full of eggs,
and smiled.

"Good morning." She gave the skillet a little shake and the eggs jounced about.

"Good morning."

I took my usual seat and watched as Mrs. Kelly spooned breakfast onto my plate. She was chipper, even for her usual self. Mr. Kelly still hadn't looked up.

Swallowing, I determined to dive right in. "Um…"

Mrs. Kelly raised her eyebrows at me. "Yes, dear?"

My words caught in my throat. The pleasant expression on her face made me doubt myself. I looked from her to Mr. Kelly, and back, confused. Was I crazy, or had last night's mood completely disappeared? It was as if it were any other day at the Kelly household.

"Nothing," I said, picking up my fork.

Furtively, I watched my foster parents eat. I waited for somebody to say something about Becky, or Sherry's visit, but nobody did. When Mrs. Kelly got up to do the dishes, she actually started humming.

"Do you want some help with those, ma'am?" I asked. I'd been pitching in with the dishes most mornings since the end of school.

"No, dear, you run along and enjoy the day." Enjoy the day?

"Um, okay." Stiffly, I stood up and headed toward the hall

like someone in a daze. Then, just as I turned the corner, I stopped myself. I didn't want to put things off another moment. I wanted us to get the talk over with now. I padded back around the corner.

But something froze me, again. There was no denying it. The scene before me was absolutely tranquil. The Kellys—both of them—couldn't have looked more content. There was no hint of worry, or anxiety, or nervousness about a big talk we should be having. There was not even the hint of a big talk to come.

Could it be that the Kellys didn't even think my leaving was worth a conversation?

As I watched from my spot by the wall, unnoticed, a look passed between them. Mrs. Kelly craned her neck back from the sink toward Mr. Kelly, and they stared at each other silently, just for a second. It was a look that clearly wasn't meant for me. It said they were in something together, just the two of them. And it was clear as day I was on the outside. The outside of their family, I guessed. They were two—and I was only one.

I dragged on up the stairs, suddenly sleepy. Alone. I guess I should have been used to that by now.

It went on the same way for the next couple of days. We'd be sitting there, watching television or eating dinner, and I'd brace myself to say something about getting adopted, but then I'd lose my nerve. It would have been hard enough as it was, but the peaceful looks on the Kellys' faces, the way they went on as if all was right with the world, made my eyes sting enough that I was scared to say anything, for fear I'd cry.

I couldn't help it. The fact that they took it so easy just kept on surprising me. They acted the same as always, if a little more quiet. Certainly not like they were losing anything they might miss. And I couldn't help my feelings being hurt. It was dumb, I knew, to expect to be worth something to them, when I knew I wasn't worth much in general. I had just thought things were different.

"Glory, why don't you come down and play a board game with us?" Mrs. Kelly poked her head into my bedroom to ask, the second night. I'd been lying on my bed, thinking. If I went to live with the Aidens, would they take care of my health the way the Kellys did? Would they take me to doctors and try to get me fixed? Maybe they didn't have the same kind of doctors. Maybe they didn't have the money.

Mrs. Kelly's figure in the doorway pulled me out of my brooding. She looked hopeful, like she was eager to have me come down and play. I didn't get her. I didn't get anything.

"No thanks, ma'am," I said, trying to summon up as much politeness as I could. What I really felt like doing was asking her why she didn't want me.

She looked disappointed for a moment, but then nodded sweetly and closed the door. Apparently we might never talk— *really* talk—at all.

With Becky, I didn't have as much of an excuse for keeping quiet. I knew I should be calling her. I even knew she wanted me to. I just didn't.

Tomorrow, I kept thinking, on both scores. Tomorrow I would bring it up. As if I had all the days in the world.

And maybe I did. It was easy to pretend, anyway; I felt fine. The summer had begun to show signs of winding down, much earlier than it ever had back home. Here it was only August, and the days weren't quite as hot as they had been. It made my heart sink that the season had gone by so fast, and that fall was just around the corner. But it was promising, that I would be making it to September, when I'd had this feeling I wouldn't.

I'd vowed to myself I wouldn't go to the pool anymore, on account of the trouble with Joe. But after a couple days of sitting home with the Kellys feeling tense, I figured maybe the embarrassment and stress at the pool wasn't so bad. It was the only place the Kellys would leave me for a while. And even if I sat on a bench and didn't swim, it would be a welcome break.

So Tuesday morning Mr. Kelly dropped me off. The kids were in the middle of Sharks and Minnows again. I scanned the group for Joe or Sadie, and saw both of them standing together, poised to jump. With a toss of her ponytail, Sadie looked over her shoulder and waved at me. Then came the signal, and in they went.

I put my pool bag down on a bench and sat beside it, pulling out a book I'd brought—*Jane Eyre*. Mr. Kelly was supposed to be back in two hours. If I just sat here and read until then, Joe and I would stay out of each other's hair and it wouldn't be so bad.

I lost track of time for a while, struggling through my story but also enthralled by it. I was just finishing a very difficult passage when I heard a commotion at the deep end of the pool.

Snapping my head up, I saw that everyone had gathered in a knot at the far left corner. Some kids were kneeling at the water's edge and some were standing with their hands over their mouths. They were all gaping down into the water. The hair on the back of my neck stood up.

I was at the edge of the pool in a second, my book forgotten. There was an empty space on the opposite corner, and I hurried to the spot, staring into the water like everybody else. The water was wavy, lapping against the edges, but peaceful looking. Except there were two shapes looming underneath it. And one shape bore the other up, until both had surfaced, and I could see them clearly. It was the lifeguard, with…

Oh God.

One of the kids let out a scream, but I didn't look up. I was mesmerized by the girl. Her face was pale white and her cheeks seemed to be sucking in. Her body lolled in the lifeguard's arms. And then I saw the blood streaming out behind them, seeming to flow out of the tips of her long black hair.

Before I could think, before I could even breathe, they were right in front of me, and he was saying something.

"…nine-one-one!"

"Uh…" I sputtered. I didn't understand. I couldn't think. I couldn't feel my body.

"Call nine-one-one!" he screamed, this time angry. All I could do was stare at him in confusion. Some kids had come running up behind me, and now one of them seemed to get the message. He ran off with me still wondering, *What was 911?*

In a blink, the lifeguard had hoisted the girl onto the tiles beside me, and then he was out and leaning over her, dripping all over her. Miraculously, her eyes were open now. He grabbed a towel and gently tucked it under her head.

My eyes glazed over. I felt like I was going blind, and I blinked upward to clear them. Just then a pair of eyes met mine from across the circle. It took me a moment to place Joe. While everyone else's eyes were on the pair on the floor, his eyes were on me.

I looked back down, ashamed. So much shame and regret came over me that I felt it might knock me over. I had done this. Somehow, I was responsible.

The girl was crying, but quietly. Her eyelids were all scrunched up in pain. The lifeguard had a second towel pressed against the top of her forehead, just at the hairline, and was I imagining it or did the bleeding seem to be slowing down?

"You're gonna be fine," he was saying to her. "Do you hear me? You're going to be fine. Maybe a concussion…"

I swallowed, and stared. Was he lying? Was he just saying that?

Then the girl, ever so slightly, nodded. And made a grimace that seemed meant to be a smile.

The feeling in the room was powerful enough that I could sense something had changed. Fear had become relief, or something close to it. Kids were now talking to one another nervously, one girl was holding the wounded girl's hand and saying soothing things. But there was no panic or terror anymore. It all happened so quickly, making me feel even more bewildered.

And then the double doors of the hall came roaring open, and several men—they looked like police almost—rushed in carrying a bed of some sort, like the kind you see at a hospital. Lights flashed behind them as the doors squealed closed.

They worked quickly, securing the girl to the bed with all sorts of straps, asking her questions, looking at the cut on her head, which, I could see clearly now, was not terribly big. They were serious and concerned, but not panicked. In another few moments, they were carrying her outside.

"She's going to be all right, everybody." The lifeguard was standing now, his arms raised to get the crowd's attention. "Everything's fine."

A mutter went up from the kids, and then they began to mill about, some even getting back into the pool.

But I couldn't move. My heart was thumping so hard I thought it might burst.

I stared at the water, or into the water, or maybe *past* the water. The blood in my temples felt too thick for the veins, just pounding and pounding away.

"Glory?"

I looked up. It was Joe, his hands on his hips in his usual

way, only he was looking at me, talking to me, with some hint of the old Joe who cared.

"Glory, are you okay?"

I didn't say anything. I just nodded. Then he was gone, and for all I knew he could have vanished into thin air. The world was spinning. Or was it me who was spinning?

All I saw was a bucket filled with water, only the bucket was me and there were all these holes. Everything inside me flowed out, but I never got empty. The more I seeped through all those holes, the more water appeared. And somewhere in the bottom of the bucket I saw the thought and not the feeling: Katie. There was no forgetting. I was responsible.

All I knew was that I wanted to get away from the pool and what had happened there. I headed straight for the doors, hoping that no one was looking at me. In a split second, I had the door handle in my hands. Then I was outside, halfway across the lot. I was going to walk home.

"Glory!"

He was hurrying toward me, not quite running. Then he was next to me and gripping my arm. Joe. Dear friend Joe. "Bye," I said, feeling the ground sucking at my feet. I couldn't imagine why, but I started laughing—I think it was because his eyes were so big and surprised. My eyelids came down like walls over my eyes, and the last thing I saw was his face as I fell. Poor Joe. He looked like he had seen a ghost.

This is it.

It was almost like I'd pictured it. I was hooked up to some tubes again. A machine was bleeping behind my bed. I felt weak and withered, inside and out.

It was almost the vision I'd had when picturing my final days.

Except.

Except I hadn't expected to feel so calm. I hadn't expected to *want* to give in. I hadn't expected to stop caring whether I made it to a year or not, and in fact being almost relieved I hadn't. Lance King had made it only weeks after he was cast out, only to be found dead in the woods. I'd traveled hundreds of miles, I'd lived for months. It was enough.

In my mind, death was a shadowy person, standing in my hospital room, waiting for me to leave with him. I wanted to invite him in, have him sit down with me, feel welcome. At least he was someone I could count on. But there was a little part of me that resisted that. I wanted to stay awake and see...I don't know. I wanted to see the end...if that makes any sense.

The doctors had been in and out, in and out. They didn't ask me if I was ready to die. They just looked at the facts—that my heart beat a slow, crazy rhythm, that my body wasn't doing what it was supposed to.

"Your autonomic nervous system isn't functioning properly, and we're trying to pinpoint why." "You don't retain fluids properly." All of it meant nothing to me. The Kellys seemed to take them more seriously, asking lots of questions, nodding solemnly at the answers.

I considered telling them not to bother, as if it would make any difference. I thought maybe I should tell them there was no escaping memories of Katie, and I was responsible for everything, and there was no point trying to push them deeper inside of me, and they should just let me alone.

At the pool, before I'd collapsed, I'd thought of myself as a bucket, leaking. And that was true: I couldn't stop the leaking—all that sadness about Katie and home flowing out of me. There *was* peace and happiness in the world, I guessed, but they were for somebody else, not for me.

"We're going to be keeping you for a while," a doctor, whose name I didn't know, told us that first night. Mr. Kelly looked disappointed, but to me it was no surprise. We watched the doctor leave in awkward silence.

Mrs. Kelly had gone home for the night, after dropping off a bag of clothes for me. Mr. Kelly had insisted on staying, though I'd sworn up and down I didn't need him to. I knew he was only doing it out of kindness, and that he'd have been more comfortable at home with his wife. But I hadn't been able to talk him out of it. He sat down on the chair near my bed and looked at his hands. I looked at mine.

The bed had a little remote control attached to it, and I finally turned on the television, flicking endlessly through the channels. "Hey, look at that guy's hair," I said, smiling at Mr. Kelly. "It looks like a skunk fell asleep on his head."

I wanted to cheer him up, take his mind off things. But he only aimed a polite smile at me. I wished I could make him look the other way from it all. It didn't even hurt anymore that he and Mrs. Kelly were willing to let me go off to the Aidens. I just wished I'd gone sooner so I could be out of their hair.

"I told you," I said suddenly, trying to look wry. "I told you I was a burden."

He didn't find it funny. "And I told you you weren't."

I swallowed, feeling like it had been a stupid thing to say as a joke.

Mr. Kelly met my eyes sympathetically, then huffed. "You know, maybe we haven't made that clear enough to you. Sometimes I have trouble saying the things I should."

I hesitated. "Like not saying anything about me getting adopted?" I asked, hoping I wasn't too bold. "By the Aidens?" There was nothing to lose now, I figured. We could clear the air once and for all. It might make the Kellys feel better. Still, I had to struggle to hide the lump in my throat.

"You know," I continued, "it's okay. You're only my foster parents. It's not like…you ever said you'd…adopt me, or anything. And you know, I would have been happy with the Aidens…"

"*Would* have?" he asked.

I pushed past it. "I just don't want you to feel bad, for"—I cleared my throat—"not wanting to keep me."

Mr. Kelly's eyes widened, then his gray eyebrows nestled down right over his eyelids, his forehead bunching up into deep wrinkles. He slapped one hand to his eyes, then shook his head, smiling ruefully.

"I told her. I told her we should say something."

"Say what?" I asked, bewildered.

My body felt like a lump of mush, but I had enough energy to frown deep and big. I hated feeling so ignorant.

Finally Mr. Kelly seemed to notice my look because he turned serious. "Glory, it's the opposite. We *wanted* to adopt you, we've always had that in mind, even before we met you."

He shrugged helplessly. "But we thought...Oh, the Aiden thing took us by surprise. And then...Caroline thought we should let you bring it up when you were ready. She said we shouldn't influence your decision."

"What?" I felt my face heating up. The monitor that was hooked up to my finger started beeping to the faster rhythm of my heart.

"We wanted you to know we'd be all right if you left. We didn't want to make you feel bad, if you wanted to go to the Aidens. I know you have a relationship with them..."

"But..." I sputtered, "...but that's...how could I make a decision if I didn't even know you would adopt me?" Suddenly I was angry and happy and thankful at the same time.

"I didn't say it was a good plan." He paused, staring out the window beyond my bed, then focusing on me again. "It wasn't the smartest way to handle it, I guess."

I felt the familiar sting under my eyelids. Darn it, I was going to cry.

"Mr. Kelly, may I have some time alone please?"

He looked surprised, but said, "Sure." He paused. "I'm sorry, you must need your rest. I'll be back in the morning, okay?"

I nodded, trying my best to give him a reassuring smile.

When he was gone I pulled my pillow over my face and

breathed into it, letting my tears soak into the cloth. Why did everything in this world hurt so much? Why did I have to care about the Kellys and why did they have to care about me? They wanted me after all. They wanted me, and I hadn't seen it.

It was too much for me to bear. I felt trapped by all the tubes and wires stuck to me. I felt homesick and scared. And it hurt, to be cared for. Bad, terrible old me.

The door opened and I pulled the pillow off my face, sitting up to see one of the nurses. "Just need to get some blood," she said, leaning over my arm. Once she'd filled the little glass vial, she looked at my face, and saw that I'd been crying.

"Now," she said, patting my shoulder sympathetically. "Now, now. Don't worry. You'll be out of here in no time."

I thought I caught a shadow behind her, and nodded, agreeing. If Death really was a person, I imagined he'd just sat down, taken off his hat, and made himself right at home.

CHAPTER
SEVEN

It was late in the night when the door cracked open. I'd been sleeping, dreaming, I guess, and the squeak of the door barely reached me. It was the skin-prickling feeling that I was being watched that pulled me awake. Had Mr. Kelly come back after all? My eyes opened to a pair of legs, and then traveled upward to meet the eyes of Joe Trew.

"Good Lord!" I breathed, sitting straight up and pulling against the covers. What was he doing here?

"Shhh." He raised his finger to his lips, then looked back toward the door, which stood open behind him. He seemed not to know whether he should shut it or not. He fidgeted back and forth on his feet, looked at me and back, then took hold of the knob and pushed it closed. He came back to the edge of my bed. Hanging from his left arm was my swim bag. He set it down against a wall.

"I wasn't spying, I just...you were so peaceful and I didn't want to…" He looked guilty, and a little nervous.

I swallowed, hardly paying attention to his words. A hot ball of fire had come to life in my stomach—what was he doing here?

He spoke barely above a whisper. "I came to see how you were doing. It's past visiting hours, but there's a staircase that…where you don't have to go past the front desk." He stepped closer, staring at his hands. I stared at them, too, unable to look at his face. "I was worried about you."

"Oh," I managed to choke. Worried about me? "Um." And then I remembered my looks must be a fright. My skin was about the color of my hospital robe, and my hair felt greasy and tangled. I smoothed at it a bit, then stopped myself.

Wait a second here. What was I doing, sitting in my hospital bed and worried about how I looked for Joe? Wasn't he the one who'd ignored my calls and made going to the pool so miserable for me? Okay, so I'd deserved it. But still. It had *hurt*.

"I'm fine, thank you." I was as polite as I could be without sounding friendly. I crossed my arms over my ugly robe.

Joe eyed me, his head tilted to one side. Then he nodded. "Okay, well…um…" He seemed on the verge of running out of the room. *Please don't* was all I could think. But my pride wouldn't let me say it.

He shifted from foot to foot, turned to look at the door again. Then he seemed to come to a decision. His jaw set. "I don't—" he began, then stopped, then began again. "I don't want it to be like this."

"Like what?" I asked, fake casually.

"Like this. We both want to be friends, I think..." His eyebrows rose at this. "But we just won't say it. I don't want it like that."

I gulped, crossing my arms tighter. "Well. Well, I don't either."

"Me neither."

"Good."

"Yep."

We stared at each other. I felt so uncomfortable I wanted to cry. We held each other's gaze long enough that one of us should have looked away, but neither of us did. And soon I started to feel embarrassed. And it brought this nervous smile to my face. After a second, the corners of Joe's lips followed. And then he started cracking up, and I did, too, in this nervous, happy, giddy way.

"May I approach the throne?" he asked, shyly waving at my bed with his arm.

I nodded. "You may."

Without meeting my eyes again, he perched sheepishly on the edge of the bed.

"So…" he asked, "what did I do?"

Oh Lord. The question broke my heart. His voice was sorry and sad and angry all at once.

I shook my head furiously. "Nothing. You didn't do a thing. It's just my life is—it's just… Gosh, I'm so sorry."

"Nothing?" Joe asked, peering at me from underneath his eyebrows in that earnest way I loved.

I shook my head again.

He let his gaze fall downward and kept it there, as if he were looking at something very interesting, and then his hand slid to the side, toward mine. Finally he took it gently in his and pulled it closer to him. Then he met my eyes again.

"Was it because of this? At the church that day?" He swallowed, hard, so that his Adam's apple bobbed up and down. "Do you not want me to hold your hand?"

I couldn't believe it. I felt like my spirit was spinning and spinning inside. Wherever his hand was touching mine, a million tiny shocks went off. I didn't even look down. Ridiculously, I pretended like I didn't notice.

"Well. Um, it doesn't matter," I said stupidly. "I mean, it wasn't that. I mean, I want us to be friends."

"Yeah, friends…" Joe said, pulling his hand away. "Me, too."

Oh no. Had I said the wrong thing? I had to fix it.

"Like…like you and Sadie," I said. "Like, if you guys are, more than friends, you can tell me, you know."

Joe looked startled for a moment, and then shook his head.

"Oh, God no. No, Sadie and I are old friends. She has a huge crush on Neil. They have a huge crush on each other. But she'd kill me if I told."

"Oh?" Ridiculously, a laugh threatened to bubble out of me. "Maybe they should tell each other," I muttered.

"Maybe," Joe said.

We sat for another moment, my heart feeling like it was going to pop out of my body. Joe touched my hand again, and his thumb began patting my skin, lightly. He tightened his fingers around mine.

And then I couldn't keep it in—I just burst out giggling.

"What?" he asked.

"Nothing."

"C'mon, tell me."

"Nothing. I'm just…nervous." My hand, as if it had a mind of its own, rose to his shoulder and picked some lint from his T-shirt. It stayed there, boldly, against his arm. He smiled.

"Don't be nervous." And then he leaned toward me, and I

closed my eyes. And when his lips touched mine I felt like I was on another planet—that this couldn't be happening. That I, Glory Mason, could be kissing someone.

When Joe backed away and looked at me again, we both had huge, goofy grins on our faces. He gave me a playful, embarrassed shove on the arm. His face was bright red, and I imagined mine was, too.

"Scoot over," he said. "You still owe me some info."

He was right. I did. So I scooted and he sat beside me, and he held my hand. And then I told him everything. Every single thing.

And believe it or not, it felt good to tell it.

Joe was completely, utterly silent. From the part where I got to Katie's dying onward, he didn't say one word. I would have figured he'd hate me, but he only squeezed my hand tighter and tighter. When I talked about Doc bending over Katie, and letting us know she was gone, he simply wrapped his arms around me—a bit unsurely and awkwardly—and patted my back. When I talked about the Water of Judgment, he squeezed my fingers so tight I thought he was going to break them off, and his eyes were huge.

It was strange, how much I trusted Joe. I'd thought I trusted Becky, and Jake, and the Kellys, but there were parts of me I'd always kept from them. Even at home, I'd never felt perfectly understood around anyone. Except for Katie, that is. And when I thought of that, I realized Joe was now my best friend.

It made me feel guilty, as if Katie had been replaced. But then I pictured her, clearer than I had in a long while, being happy for me. She would have wanted me to have a best friend, I knew it. Especially someone as kind and caring as Joe. And she would have understood she could never be replaced.

We sat there for a long time after I was done, until I couldn't stand it anymore. I wanted to know what he *thought*.

"So?" I asked.

Joe stared at me for a long moment. "Glory, I don't know what to say."

"Well…tell me…anything. You're the first person I ever told…all of it to."

"That just makes it harder. I don't know enough about anything to help you."

"Yeah," I said. "Well, it can't be helped. It just feels good that you know." It wasn't like he could work miracles, I knew. I stared down at the blankets.

"The poison, I don't know. It just sounds so crazy. You say that's how they punish people?"

I nodded. "It's always been that way."

"I can't imagine," he said. "The thing is, you still…you still sound like you think you're a bad person, or something. Like you deserve all this…horrible stuff. I mean, it's all really horrible what's happened. I just…"

"Well, the Reverend always said you lie in the bed you've made. I'm the one that broke the rules and got Katie killed."

"No."

"No?"

"I mean, you're looking at it in such a weird way. I mean, what happened was really, um, really *unlucky*. I mean, people do bad things. They make mistakes. That's being a human being. What happened to you was a mistake. What you did wasn't so wrong, Glory, it was just a mistake. What happened, it was bigger than anything you did."

Joe removed his hand from mine and kneaded it together with his other, frustrated.

"Joe, you may look at it that way. But you don't understand. You don't see that what I did by drinking spirits was a sin. You don't believe in God and—"

"You said *you* don't believe in God anymore."

"Well…"

"And anyway, I believe in God. I mean, maybe not an old guy with a beard who sits on the clouds and decides to let good and bad things happen. But I believe in *something*. I believe somebody is watching over us. And I *know* God wouldn't want you to feel this way. I know you're wrong about yourself. You're the best person I've ever met, and you think you're the worst."

"Well…" I had nothing to say to Joe. I couldn't find a way to get around his words.

"And those people, back in your home. They may be good people, but, what they did to you was really wrong. Maybe they thought they were doing right and all of that, but can't you see they weren't?"

My head ached. I couldn't even understand what Joe was saying, not really. About some God who wasn't God, and how folks in Dogwood were different, not wrong. My daddy wouldn't have let them poison me, if it wasn't the right thing…

"When that girl got hurt at the pool, it reminded you of Katie."

This, at least, I could understand. I nodded.

"Katie's gone, you know."

"I know."

"Yeah, I know you know, but maybe in a way, you don't. Back in California, my grandpa was like my second dad. He even lived with us. When he died"—Joe's voice became deep and low—"I knew he was dead, but in a way I kept hoping he'd come back…by magic or something. And I guess hoping is usually good, but sometimes, it just keeps you from getting over things."

"But I'm not hoping Katie's coming back," I muttered. "I know she's not."

Joe sighed. "I know. It's just, somehow…it's like you think you should die with her."

The clock on the wall showed it was past two o'clock in the morning. Joe's eyes were wide and weary. I felt bad for keeping him up so late.

"It doesn't matter," I said. "I can't help but die and—"

"*Don't* say that Glory. You're not going to die. The doctors will fix it. I'm telling you."

I nodded. *No, they won't.*

"You should get home," I said, smiling at Joe sympathetically.

"You're not gonna die," he said again, truly meaning it. He put an arm around my shoulder and let me lean against him. As we talked, I could feel the rumble of his voice against my cheek, and it soothed me. Soon I was drifting off, in and out of sleep.

Gently, he stood up and brushed himself off. "I'm gonna let you get some rest," he said. "Good night, Glory."

"Good night," I whispered, suddenly fearful. He was leaving. And what reason did he have to come back? Who would possibly like a girl with so many problems?

But as he left, he scooped down and put his lips on mine, just for a second. It felt as good as before. My skin tingled everywhere, and at the same time I felt all warm and reassured inside. But it also made my heart ache. I was terribly afraid I'd never see him again.

I stared at the clock, watching the minutes tick by: 2:36, 2:37, 2:38. My stomach hurt, way down deep inside. I looked around the room. Instead of freeing me to go to sleep, Joe's leaving had made me wide-awake. Now I was just staring at all the gadgets—screens, lights, knobs, switches—helplessly. White walls, big wide windows looking out on other walls across the way. I couldn't stand the smell of my room. Nothing about it was natural, or deep, or thick the way life smells are. It smelled like emptiness. Home had smelled like jasmine and turned earth and dry leaves and baking. I wanted to smell it again.

No, Glory.

I'd been having the most foolish thoughts. What Joe had said had been running circles through my mind and coming back to the same idea—I needed to get out of here. I could get out of my bed, pack my things, and...

It was crazy. I tried to think about other things. But I couldn't shake the thought of leaving, going home.

They would all forgive me, right? If I left?

No. No no no. You wouldn't make it, Glory. You'd drop somewhere, and that would be the end of it. You'd die all alone.

Still, I sat up and swiveled my legs so that they hung off the side of the bed, which made the tube in my arm pull at my skin. I examined it closely, then tugged at the tape until it came off. I pulled the needle out of my arm and, seeing what I'd done, I felt my stomach ache harder. I stood up.

Gol. My head swam, and then cleared.

My pool bag was against the wall, and looking at it, I made a deal with myself. If my money was still in it, I'd do what I was thinking of doing. Twenty dollars would be enough to buy me some food and other things I needed. But if it wasn't in there anymore, I'd stay. I'd take it as a sign—though from who, I didn't imagine.

Quietly, as if I'd already done something wrong, I unzipped the side pocket of the bag, sliding my hand into it. And there, crisp and folded twice, was my twenty-dollar bill.

My body moved without my brain, silently and quickly. I feared somebody, one of the nurses maybe, might be reading my mind. But nobody came in to check on me, not as I slowly pulled on my shorts and a T-shirt Mrs. Kelly had brought. Not even when I went into the tiny bathroom and splashed my face, trying to get some color back into it, trying to wake myself up. I swayed on my feet a little. I wanted to rest. But I wasn't going to rest here. Rest would come later, not now.

I opened my knapsack and collected my toothbrush, toothpaste, nail clippers, and a washcloth (also brought by Mrs. Kelly), and tucked them inside. I knew there were already a few pairs of underwear and two pairs of comfy pants inside, as well as a few more T-shirts.

Finally, feeling like I was in a dream, I searched the room for a pen and something to write on. Both were in a drawer beside my bed. The white paper, like the pen, had the words *Boston Mercy Hospital* across the top.

Dear Mr. and Mrs. Kelly, I scribbled, and stopped. What to say? *Thank you for everything.* That didn't sound right. *I will always be grateful*...I scratched out both lines, nibbled on the pen, and then finally wrote, *I am so lucky I met you. Thank you for everything.* It wasn't good enough, but it would have to do. I signed my name, then folded the paper, leaving it beside the bed in clear view.

The note for Joe was easier. I told him what a good friend he was, and I said that I hoped he'd understand. I truly believed, now that he knew everything, he would.

I hoisted my knapsack over my shoulder.

I suppose there were a lot of second thoughts going through my mind. I searched the room, making sure I'd remembered everything (not that there was much to remember). Maybe I was wrong. Maybe I shouldn't do this. And I thought, would Joe really understand after all? Would the Kellys be okay with me gone?

But none of the doubts were enough to stop me. It was like one thought had taken over my brain, and if I didn't obey it I'd be lost. I needed to do this more than I'd ever needed anything in my life.

I needed to go back to Dogwood. I needed to go home.

CHAPTER
EIGHT

I stood on the side of the highway, my thumb hooked out like I'd seen on TV. It was drizzling slightly, a cool summer rain that was airy and soft.

It had been a long, dangerous walk from the hospital to the highway, down several blocks and then a curved ramp that was busy with cars, even at this late hour. I knew it was even more dangerous to be standing here, trying to get a ride from a stranger. But I told myself I didn't have much to lose.

Despite all the cars, it took a good half an hour before somebody stopped. A small red car pulled up about fifty yards past me. Swallowing, I squinted at it, making sure it was waiting for me. Then I jogged up and lowered my head to the window.

To my relief, the driver was a woman.

"Are you crazy?" she asked, pushing the door open as she did so. I slid inside, suddenly sheepish. "How long do you think you can stand out there before some lunatic comes along?"

I didn't know what to say. The woman had a deep northern accent and talked in harsh, clipped tones. I sat, too shocked to answer. She was *scolding* me. Luckily, she didn't seem to expect a reply.

"You're lucky it was me and not somebody else, that's all I can say."

"Yes, ma'am," I murmured. "I really appreciate it."

The car was in motion now and the woman seemed to calm down. "Where are you headed?" she asked, giving me a quick look-see. She had long, curly brown hair.

"I was hoping...could you drop me off at the nearest truck stop?"

This seemed to take her by surprise. She shook her head in a gesture that said, "I can't believe it."

Fear ran up and down my veins, like melting ice. What if she decided to call the police about me, thinking I was a runaway? How could I not have thought of that, especially after all I'd been through? "I'm meeting someone there," I blurted out, desperately. "My daddy. He's a trucker."

Eyeing her profile, I could tell she didn't believe me. "He...he and my mama don't get along and she won't drive me to see him. But you know, he's my daddy. And he called to say he was passing through."

I didn't know where the words were coming from, or where I could've gotten such a story. I couldn't picture my own daddy as a trucker, but I tried to summon up the feelings I'd have if I were about to see him again. It wasn't hard, considering I might.

"I can't wait to see him," I said, "I've missed him so much."

Again, I watched the lady for her reaction. I had to admit, the catch in my voice was convincing. She shrugged.

"It's your life," she said, her eyes on the road. I breathed a little easier after that.

When the car pulled off of the highway and into a large, well-lit parking lot, the clock read 4:34.

"Thank you so much," I said, setting a foot outside the door and gathering up my knapsack.

The driver nodded. "Be careful out there," she warned. And that was it.

"Yes, ma'am." I nodded. "Thank you again."

"Take care," she said, before I slammed the door. Her car made a swishing sound as she drove off.

Phew. I blew my wet hair out of my face and looked heavenward. I couldn't believe the sun wasn't up yet and I was already out of Boston. Could I really be outside of Boston? I looked behind me as if to make sure it was true, but all I could see was night. Already, packing up my things in the hospital, and sneaking down the back stairs Joe had told me about, seemed like something somebody else had done. Not me. Not Glory Mason.

I could feel myself blushing, though, remembering how it felt when Joe had kissed me. *That* was real. And then, here I was, living proof of everything else.

I felt like I'd just leaped from a cliff.

But this was right where I wanted to be, I was sure of it. On my way home, to the mountains! I could smell the country air already. If I could just set foot in the Appalachians, get a glimpse of home, it would be the dearest day of my life.

I turned toward the building at the far end of the lot and started walking, keeping an eye on the trucks and cars that zig-zagged across the pavement. The place was so busy, you'd think it was lunchtime rather than five in the morning. But judging by its size, I could see why. The place was huge, with a restaurant on one side and a shop on the other. It seemed the perfect, welcome sight for lonely people who may have been up all night, or maybe just getting up. It was so brightly lit it was almost mesmerizing, and it was filled with people, which made it all the more inviting.

I walked into the restaurant, gazing about. Men, I realized. I hadn't noticed from the outside, but the place was full of men. A few of them looked so much like Mr. Aiden that I had to do a double take. I wondered if they were mostly truckers, and decided they were.

"Table or counter?" A woman stood in front of me, a big plastic menu in her hands. A waitress.

"Um..." I cast about to see what the difference was. "Counter?" Without a word she turned and began walking, and not knowing what I was supposed to do, I followed. She stopped at a long counter, speckled white, with a tall red chair before it, and waited for me to sit down. I climbed up on the chair, feeling so self-conscious that I almost fell off.

"Whoa," she said, holding out a hand to keep me upright. "You know what you want?"

"Um, no, ma'am."

"All right, I'll be back in a few." She handed me the menu and started away, but then stopped and backtracked, eyeing me strangely. "You here with someone?"

I nodded deeply. "Oh yes, it's just...my daddy already ate," I said, hooking a finger back toward the parking lot. I looked back down at the menu quickly, flipping through it as if I didn't have a care in the world. Out of the corner of my eye I could see her shrug and then walk away.

The menu was four pages long and listed all sorts of things, including eggs fixed in more ways than you could shake a stick at. I searched for something cheap and filling—and finally ordered plain old scrambled eggs. Coffee would have been nice, to help warm me and wake me up, but I didn't want to pay the extra money.

I was dazed while I waited for my meal, and stayed that way while I ate it. But when I'd finished, and my aching stomach was soothed, I started fidgeting, looking around. The food had made me wide-awake, and now it really sunk in where I was and what I'd done.

I'd snuck out of the hospital. I'd left the Kellys and Joe behind. I was going home.

The last realization was so strange that I still couldn't get myself to believe it. I wouldn't believe it till I saw the tip of the very first village house, so impossible did it seem. For now, I had to focus on one thing at a time, or I was likely to be over-whelmed.

I counted out my bill money and laid it on the counter, then glanced about the room, wondering who I would approach first. There were a few women scattered about, and I figured I'd rather try my luck with them first. I looked to make sure my waitress wasn't around, in case she might get more suspicious, and then settled on a woman who had corn yellow hair, streaked with brown. I stood up and wove my way among the tables toward her.

"Excuse me?"

The woman looked up, without surprise or interest.

"Are you driving south, by any chance?"

"Nope," she said, eating another forkful of food. Just like that.

"Oh," I said. "Thanks."

Flustered, I turned to the person two chairs over—a man with a beard, because I thought he might have overheard anyway. "Excuse me, sir? Are you headed south by any chance?"

He shook his head, but looked at me more curiously than the first lady. I moved on quickly.

It took three tries before I found someone headed south, and six before I found someone who had heard of Shadow Tree, West Virginia, and had it on their route. Each time I had to ask someone new, I felt more antsy. I felt like more and more eyes were on me, maybe wondering why I was here and if I belonged.

But thankfully, the man going to Shadow Tree agreed to take me. I didn't want to go all the way there, I explained, but to stop a little before (there wasn't much point mentioning Dogwood;

it surely wasn't on any map). I made a point of saying that my parents lived at the end of a dirt road, and that I could walk from there.

"That's fine," the man said. He didn't seem to care either way, though he had a kind look about him that made me feel comforted. How I would know exactly *where* to stop, I did not know. But I certainly wasn't going to mention that. I'd just have to figure it out somehow. If worse came to worse, I would get to Shadow Tree then turn around and make my way back until I found the right road. The one that Jake had driven me down that morning, on my way out into the world.

The truck driver introduced himself as Chuck Martin, and said he'd be ready to leave in about an hour and to meet him at the entrance. Relieved, I went off on my own to the store opposite the restaurant, as much to get away from the restaurant as to buy some much needed supplies. I was starting to feel like I stood out too much. In any case, the sooner we got away from here, the safer I'd feel.

I loaded my arms with cheap, filling types of food that would be easy to carry—peanut butter crackers, a block of cheese, beef jerky that came in little clear wrappings. I bought matches, and avoided anything canned. I had learned to be more practical than that.

Within a few minutes I was all set. I loaded everything into my knapsack then went into the bathroom and washed my face. Finally I settled on a bench outside the restaurant entrance with half an hour left.

It was still drizzling, and I lifted my face up, appreciating the wetness against my skin. I could have missed out on this, I thought. I could have stayed locked up in that hospital for the rest of my days. A feeling of relief and emotion so huge swept over me, I was almost in tears.

The sun was just beginning to rise, though it couldn't be seen. I knew it was morning by the dimmest light that had now spread over the trees. I leaned my head against my left shoulder. Had the hospital folks come to check on me yet, and realized I was gone? Had they called the Kellys?

Oh gosh. Suddenly I couldn't believe what I'd done. There was no turning back now, was there? Maybe if I hurried...

I stood up and walked out into the lot, ready to find a car that would take me back to the city. I couldn't leave, what had I been thinking of? Guilt made my stomach turn, along with the sureness that I must be half-crazy. What was I going home for! I certainly couldn't see my family, except maybe to spy them from afar. I didn't even know how to get there! What about the woods? Could I even find my way? And then there were the poor Kellys, to wake up and hear I was gone!

I must have been in my own world, because I didn't hear Chuck Martin approaching until he tapped me on the shoulder.

"Are you still coming with me?" he asked, chipper and wide-awake.

"Um." I looked to the lot, to the highway, to the restaurant, and back at him. If I turned back, that was it. I wouldn't get another chance. He had already started walking. I followed.

"Um, yes, sir."

"Okay. Well, I'm this red one over here," he said, pointing to the truck we were approaching, then slinging his bag from his shoulder around to his front. He opened his door, then thrust the bag up onto his seat. He followed, and within seconds the passenger side door was hanging open for me.

There was a little place to step on below the door. I used it to heave myself up and into my seat. Whoa, it was so high. As I looked down from the window, it seemed I must be sitting above where my head would be if I was standing on the ground.

"If you'll just close that door…" he said, indicating that I had left it wide open.

"Oh." I leaned over and pulled it shut, then slid back to the center of my seat and searched for a seat belt to strap myself in. Only then did I realize how very alone I was, with this stranger beside me, taking me all the way to West Virginia.

But my companion didn't seem to think anything of it. For him, I guessed, this was just an ordinary, run-of-the-mill day. It made me think how normally the world would go on, after I'd gone. Everything would be the same for everybody but me.

He turned the key and the truck rumbled into life. With some lever pushing and hissing from below, the truck lurched into motion. He fiddled with the car radio, landed on a song, and began humming under his breath. We pulled out of the lot, onto the highway headed south.

"So where you headed? Home? Visiting?" We'd been sitting in silence for hours, and the rain had gotten harder, tapping on the windshield. The sound of the wipers was mesmerizing, and it was hard to come out of my head enough to answer.

"Both," I said, my voice coming out in a croak. If I hadn't gotten so sleepy, I would have probably tried to answer better. But the sleepless night had caught up to me. Chuck didn't seem to mind, though, and anyway, I didn't think I had the energy to care. My head felt, once again, like it was wrapped in cotton. My body felt heavy, like it was filled with steel.

He just nodded, rubbing at his reddish beard.

There was a sign coming up, with the words WELCOME TO

NEW JERSEY. It made my heart flutter. On the bus, on the way to Boston, I had crossed through states, I supposed, but I hadn't known it when I did. Now I was in New Jersey. I wondered what made it different than, say, Massachussetts. I'd learned about states in my school in Boston, but not enough. Then fear clamped my gut.

"We didn't pass West Virginia yet, did we?"

Chuck laughed. "No, that's a few hours away, yet."

I leaned back, and smiled my relief at him.

"Don't worry," he said. "I won't let you sleep through it."

He did let me sleep, though. I kept waking up, jerking in my seat and thinking we'd gone too far, only to see him smiling at me, amused. The scenery was nice, and eventually the rain gave way to a clear, dry day—perfect to see by. Aside from a couple of bathroom stops, we drove and drove and drove.

When I woke up from a particularly long nap, Chuck was tapping my shoulder and it was just getting dark out.

Chuck had a brown paper bag in his lap and, seeing me looking at it, shrugged apologetically. "I stopped at McDonald's. I thought about waking you but…" He shrugged.

"Oh, that's all right," I said, still half-asleep.

"Anyway, we crossed the West Virginia border about an hour ago. I thought you might want to be on the lookout."

My stomach lurched. Suddenly I was wide-awake. "How far are we from Shadow Tree?" I blurted out, completely forgetting my manners.

"I'd say two hours, maybe two and a half."

"Oh." I sighed, feeling it was agony to have to wait that long. I watched in wonder over the next hour. As the sun went down, the land began to rise up, making soft hills all around us, which seemed to get bigger with each mile. These had to be foothills surrounding the Appalachians. I was dead silent, admiring how beautiful they were in the fading light.

Finally, something caught my eye. It was a sign for Shadow Tree, telling how many miles ahead it was. I rubbed at my eyes, not just because of Shadow Tree but because—

"Stop," I said, clutching the bag on my lap. "Please stop the truck!"

Chuck started, looked left to right, and pressed on the brakes. The machinery under the truck began to squeal. There was a bit of road marked off by a white line, and he pulled onto it, the tires hitting uneven ground underneath us. The truck shuddered, but then came to a stop.

"What is it?" he asked, confused but also in control.

I swallowed. Behind us, I knew, just a little ways, should be Jake's turnoff. The night Jake had driven me out of the woods, we'd seen a sign for Shadow Tree almost as soon as we'd come onto the highway, and now we'd just passed one that looked exactly like it. It had to be it. Didn't it? My insides started to tremble.

"I'm sorry," I breathed, turning to Chuck. "I just, I think this is my stop."

He looked at me, looked back at the empty road that stretched behind us, then looked at me again, and shook his head.

"The way you were yelling, I thought I'd run over some-body." He was clearly annoyed, but more astounded than anything else. "You sure you want to get off *here*?"

I hesitated, then nodded, and began gathering up my stuff. "Yeah, I think."

"You think?"

I didn't answer. I was already opening the door and climbing out. I felt like I could run the whole way to Jake's. It was when I was about to close the door that I realized I hadn't even said good-bye to Chuck, or thanked him. Swiftly, I stepped up onto the stair and leaned into the truck, wrapping my arms around whatever part of him I could reach, forgetting I had ever been scared of strangers.

"Thank you!"

Chuck looked at me like I'd grown a pair of pig's ears. I slammed the door behind me.

I suppose he had no choice but to drive off. The truck squealed and whooshed and pulled back onto the proper road, speeding up bit by bit. I stood stock-still, watching it disappear. Then the road was quiet and empty, and when I looked I could see only road and trees on either side of me.

My throat went dry. I'd been wrong this morning, about being so alone. *This*, this was alone.

I turned and began walking back the way we'd come, my feet hardly touching the ground.

CHAPTER NINE

One more river, one more river to cross. One more river. One more river to cross. I didn't sing the words out loud, but over and over in my head I thought them. It was a song we used to sing in church, about going to the great beyond, I guess. Except the only words I could remember were "one more river to cross." It went with the sound of my feet, hitting the dirt, over and over in exactly the same rhythm. I didn't know if it was helping to keep me going, or putting me to sleep. I felt like I could drop any second.

I'd turned off of the highway about an hour ago, onto this road which I'd thought was Jake's. But now, after walking so long, I wasn't sure. There was nothing but trees and more trees lining my path from what I could see, and I couldn't see much—night had fallen long ago. Still, I was beginning to get the sinking feeling that I was going the wrong way.

Had Jake's road gone on this long? Of course, the last time

I'd been on it I'd been in a car, so who knew how long it might take to walk. The road had gone from pavement to dirt about half a mile back, but again, this didn't tell me anything, because that night the road had been blanketed in snow.

At least the cloudy day had shaped up into a clear evening, enough so that the moon helped guide my way. I kept my eyes trained forward, searching. As if Jake's house might just suddenly appear any minute.

What would I do when I got there? I wondered. *If.* When I'd started out this morning, I'd had a picture in my mind, among many others, of seeing Jake and talking to him. But that was before I'd developed any kind of plan. If my time was running out (and it sure seemed to be), did I really have time to stop and visit? And did I really want to?

Jake was a nice boy. He'd been good to me when I had no one. But something told me that when I got to his house at the edge of the woods, I wouldn't want to stick around. Not when home was within my reach.

But what are you going to do if you get *home, Glory?* To the folks of Dogwood, after all, I was dead. I couldn't so much as show my face to a one of them.

Doesn't matter. It was a question I'd avoided all day, and one I didn't have to answer now. All I knew was that I had to get there. What happened after that didn't matter. *Just let me see it,* I begged, not knowing who I was begging. *Just let me see home.*

Ouch. Speaking of seeing. I stopped in my tracks, rubbing at my eyes. They had taken to watering in the past couple of hours, and now they felt puffed up and sticky.

I looked up again, frustrated. And then I squinted. It seemed that there was the faintest hint of a shape up ahead, different from the trees and rising above them. Was it…?

My feet launched into a quick beat, not quite running but faster than walking. I rushed past a stand of tall bushes and then my view opened wide, and I'd come into a clearing! And there, glowing white and pretty as I remembered, was a house—its chimney reaching just above the trees.

Thank God!

I clasped my hands in front of my face—*thank God thank God thank God.* It was Jake's, sure as I was born. I felt so grateful that I wanted to kiss the ground, or the sky, or something. And all I could do was thank God, who I didn't believe in. Maybe it was Joe's God I was thanking—I don't know.

The lights were all out—Jake and his family were surely long in bed. It was probably for the best, but it stung a little, to be so close to someone familiar, and not be able to see him. I circled to the right, remembering the layout perfectly, heading for the barn. I stumbled along over the lumpy ground until I'd reached it, and felt the worn wood of the walls.

Gosh, I remembered that smell. The main door was cracked open and the scent of old hay was drifting out of it. It brought all sorts of pictures into my head. Some of the barn back home, others of sitting here with Jake, letting him nurse me to health and prepare me for the outside world. I'd forgotten about him having freckles. I'd forgotten, even, how much I had liked him.

I stepped inside and felt my way around, coming upon the bed of fresh hay that had surely replaced the pile I'd slept in last year. I couldn't resist sinking into it, first on my knees, then shifting around to lie on my back, tucking my knapsack under my head.

I rubbed my eyes. I covered my face with my hands, then rested them over my belly. I imagined I was home, in my own barn, playing hide-and-seek in the hay.

When I opened my eyes again, it took me a moment to figure out why the light coming into the barn was so strange. And then I realized. *Light. Oh my gosh.* I went to stand, and my stomach lurched. My skin prickled, hot and cold. I felt like I hadn't slept a bit, but stepping out of the barn door confirmed it. There was a gray light growing in the sky to my left, and though there were still a few stars visible in the sky, they were fading. It was the verge of morning.

Okay. I swayed on my feet, scanning the fields over to the house for any sign of life. Nope. The windows were dark. It looked like the whole world was still sleeping but me.

"Okay," I said out loud, standing up straighter. I was sure, now. I didn't want to stick around. I needed to get going.

My knapsack was lying in the hay. As I picked it up, I remembered for the first time in a long while that Jake had given it to me. I hoisted it over my shoulders, then thought better of it and unzipped it, pulling out a hunk of cheese. I put it on again and rubbed the left strap with one hand, dazed. And then I turned and started off toward the woods.

My walk began slowly, but more because of my own tired body than the terrain. In fact, it was amazing how agreeable the traveling was, now that the woods weren't covered in snow. Already, I felt like I'd gone much farther than I'd expected in the short time I'd been walking. Not that I hadn't realized it would be easier; it had just been hard to imagine how *much* easier.

I didn't think about the fact that other animals probably thought so, too, until about fifteen minutes after I'd started, when I heard something crashing through the bushes behind me.

Bear, I thought, freezing. *Glory, you should have thought of bears!*

I whipped around, wondering if I should lie down and play dead like Daddy had told me to do in a case like this. It sure seemed like a foolish plan, but maybe…

The brush in front of me split open before I had time to decide, and when it did my hands went to my face. I couldn't believe my eyes.

"Mookie!" I cried, falling to my knees just as Jake's good old dog leaped at me. By the time I had my arms around her she was already wiping her tongue all over my face. I gave her a huge, hard hug.

"What are you doin', girl?" I said, pulling back to look deep in her brown eyes and then touching her nose with mine. "Where you goin'?" Then I looked up and beyond her, half hoping I'd see Jake. But there was no sign of him. And that was best, I knew.

"Are you here alone?" I asked. Mookie didn't answer. "I'm so glad you remembered me!"

I rubbed her back and belly for a good five minutes, truly touched. For a moment I felt loved, and not so alone. If I hadn't been so worried about time, I would have liked to stay all day.

Finally I stood up. "Well, I'll see you," I said. I could have sworn Mookie was smiling at me. And then I realized. *Oh.*

I crouched again and wrapped my arms around her. "Actually, I won't be coming back. You understand, right?" Tears started to tremble on my eyelids, but I blinked them away. I could sink, if I let myself, thinking that way. Finally I stood a second time and pointed over Mookie's head, back toward the way we'd come. "Go home," I said, trying to look like a person who should be obeyed.

But Mookie didn't even hesitate. She licked my hand once, then happily turned around and trotted on her way, not even looking back. My shoulders sagged. *Well, don't cry me any rivers.*

I looked up and found the North Star, which was almost faded from the sky, but not quite. I was using it, once again, to guide my way.

The day, and the one following it, turned out to be hot. So hot that it made me cranky—or else it was my own body rebelling against me, causing me to feel uncomfortable in my skin.

Both days, I walked until the sky was almost black, and then ate a cold meal, too tired to light a fire that I didn't really need anyway. On the third morning, I finally felt the crick in my neck from sleeping against my backpack on the hard ground. I sat up.

The motion caused my head to throb.

"Ow." I massaged my temples, picturing all my blood trying to rush through the tiny veins underneath. No wonder it hurt.

I lifted myself onto my haunches, then slowly stood. *Drat.* The sun, I saw now, was already quite high—it was maybe nine or ten.

"Drat." I scooped up my knapsack and pulled it around my shoulders. At least the weather seemed to have cooled off a bit. I checked the stick I'd carefully placed in the dirt last night, pointing me south. Then I headed over to the nearby stream I'd sighted and splashed my face.

How far had I come by now? Halfway? More? Last winter it had taken me a week or more to get from home to Jake's, but it seemed possible that I was cutting that time in half.

Yawning, I decided to get on my way without worrying about breakfast. I plucked a few black walnuts as I wove through the trees, sticking most of them in my pocket out of habit. I'd realized already that I had plenty of food to last me, but I couldn't get rid of the memory of being so hungry, the last time I was here. I couldn't resist gathering food where I saw it.

I tried to keep my path as straight as possible, though. My destination might not be easy to find and it would be even harder if I strayed east or west. I'd already made up my mind, sometime yesterday afternoon, that instead of making my way right toward Dogwood I'd try to find the old shelter—the one that I'd come to think of only as Lance King's. That way I could drop off my things there on the outskirts, and wait until nightfall to head into town.

I'd have to go in the dark, of course, now that I'd thought about it—though I wasn't sure how far Lance King's shelter was from town. I could scout if I needed to, I figured. And it couldn't be *too* big a distance. The night I was cast out, there'd been hard-driving snow, and no matter how roundabout my path might have been I couldn't have made it more than half a mile from home.

I shivered, remembering. The church, all lit up for the trial, and still lit up behind me when I'd run off into the woods. The Reverend with the Water of Judgment in a vial in his hands, just before. The flowers at the front of the church that Katie and I had nurtured—forget-me-nots, which weren't supposed to bloom in winter, but had been blooming that night, anyway. I'd thought how unfair it was, that they were still alive and thriving when Katie was dead…how *wrong*.

If Joe was right about somebody being above us, looking after us, then that somebody wouldn't have let that happen, right? That somebody wouldn't have let things get so mixed up, right?

Oh gosh, my heart ached. It comforted me to know it wouldn't ache much longer. I wouldn't be going to the Aidens after all, pretending to myself I was content when I never could be. Instead, I'd just...

Just...

Just what?

What would I do? What came after home? Go off into the woods again and die somewhere along the way?

It was strange that, though I'd come so many miles, it seemed that I'd come in a complete circle. Because hadn't I, the night I was cast out, had this very thought: that I wished I could die as quick as possible?

I sighed, my arms wrapped tightly around my chest. See? I thought, picturing Mr. and Mrs. Kelly and the hurt I'd surely caused them, and all the time I'd spent, and all the miles I'd traveled for no reason. *You might as well have saved yourself the effort, Glory. You might as well have stayed here.*

It was long past dark when I gave up walking, admitting to myself that there was no point when I could hardly see my own hand in front of my face. I settled down on the leaves, breathing in their smell, wishing I had had this with me all along. I fell asleep thinking of Katie's lake, black and shiny and still, surrounded by trees that looked like shadows, with the light falling between them as clear as diamonds. It made its way into my dreams; it went in a circle: dream after dream, after dream.

When I woke I saw that all my stumbling in the dark had not been in vain at all. Twenty feet away from where I was lying, clear through the rustling underbrush, was the shelter I'd been looking for. I could see it plain as day.

CHAPTER
TEN

Was it a miracle? Was it luck?

I approached the shelter in awe, amazed that over the whole way I'd walked, I'd somehow come to make my bed right at its front door.

I'd always thought of it as the shelter Lance King had built. But getting closer, then touching it, then bending down to look inside, I saw there were signs of me all over it—the doorway I'd propped up and fixed, the dried-up pine needles still piled inside. It wasn't in great shape, but it was still standing, and I couldn't help but take my share of pride in that. Lance and I had made something, the two of us, that would last a while longer. It was the one small thing we were leaving behind.

I turned the question over in my mind, of how I could have come upon it so easily. *Oh, who knows*, I thought, ducking down and crawling into the darkness of the shelter. I reached up to a familiar corner, just to reassure myself. There were his initials—

L.B.K. He'd been punished like me, and died here. And here I was, after running my big circle, in the same spot.

Leave it to you to do things the hard way, Glory Mason.

I pulled my knapsack inside and slowly began unpacking it, putting all the food on a makeshift shelf. I felt the loss of my family photograph—it was still in the drawer of my bureau in Boston. I wondered what I'd find changed about the Mason family, if I were lucky enough to see the real thing. Tonight, maybe, I'd find out.

For now, I had to figure out where I was, exactly. As soon as I'd had something to eat, I'd head off again, marking my path, to find out exactly how close I was to town.

I'd planned to sleep a little, just a nap, until it was late enough. But instead, that night I lay awake in my shelter, counting the minutes. The moon was bright as silver and sending a dim light through the slats of wood, making patterns on my arms and legs. I gazed at the cracks of light as long as I could stand it, then sat up, mechanically pulling on my socks and shoes. It was around midnight, I gauged. Late enough. Time.

Outside the hut, the air was clean and cool. I sucked it in. My stomach, already aching, pinched at the motion. The nerves all over my body felt like they were filled with electricity, the kind that could light up all of Boston. I felt like a spring sat coiled up in my belly. I was going home tonight.

I'd found the outskirts of town this evening by a stand of pines that had been cut down, leaving only their stumps. I'd recognized it as one of the spots where folks got their timber. I remembered it well from the times I'd gone with Daddy, and knew the way home from there.

I stretched my arms, looking about at the trees and under-brush, all rustling ever so faintly. Was I forgetting anything?

There was nothing I might need, except for my own two legs. But still, I ducked into the shelter again, to check. Just as I was pulling out, I caught a glimpse of the familiar initials, L.B.K., above my head. On an impulse, I reached up, my fingers trac-ing the letters. Where was Lance King now? Where was Katie? Did they have spirits that went to heaven? Or were the initials and memories all that were left?

Would I disappear, too?

I stuck my hand in my bag and searched around for the clip-pers I'd packed at the hospital. Then I moved my fingernails into one of the small grooves, and pulled out the sharp bit you are supposed to use for under your nails. I lifted my eyes, again, to Lance King's initials, and just below them. It took all of two minutes to scratch my own letters, G.B.M. *There.* Who knew how long this shelter would stand? A couple of years, maybe. But the bark would be around longer, lying on the ground maybe.

It wasn't enough, but it was something.

The way back to the timber yard took longer than I expected. On top of the darkness, I was as skittish as a colt. Every time a tree rustled, or a branch snapped with my passing, I froze, not moving till I was satisfied it had been nothing. And then my heart was pounding so hard that I had to walk slowly, trying to get myself calm.

All in all, it was probably an hour before I came upon the gathering of stumps—dark and crooked and spreading out for at least an acre. From here, I reckoned, it would take fifteen minutes more to reach the edge of town.

I was on familiar land now—the kind I could navigate even in the dark. My legs carried me east, where I knew I'd catch Dogwood on the Mason family side, picking up speed. I knew, also, what I'd come across this way.

It was strange, not knowing how I would feel when I saw it. I pictured myself crying, or at least sitting down to take it all in. I pictured knowing with sureness that I had arrived home.

But when the lake finally came into view, I didn't feel that I'd *arrived* anywhere. Instead I felt like I was being lifted up, up, and up—into the air, floating above it all.

The water was glassy and still. I walked right up to its edge. In the moonlight, it seemed to be black, instead of dirty brown, and inky. It seemed smaller than I remembered it; I'd always thought of it as so big. Theo and I had swum here. Thomas Johansen and I had caught fish here. Katie had died here.

Katie died here. Katie died here.

I crouched, and my arms floated in front of me toward the water. My fingertips broke the surface, sending out ripples. This was my history. It had been so long since I'd seen my history. But I couldn't get it to make sense. I couldn't get it to mean what it should, inside.

I watched the water, dazed. Where were all the feelings I was supposed to have? It was like I was watching it all on TV. Maybe if Katie had lain here for good, instead of being recovered like she was, I would have felt differently. Maybe if it were winter, and the lake was icy like it had been that night.

Try as I might, nothing came to me. *Maybe I don't even have a heart anymore,* I thought. *Maybe I'm not good enough to care.*

And then another thought came. Maybe Joe had been right, back in the hospital. Maybe I didn't really believe she was gone. But how could that be, when I *knew* that she was? I'd cried over her, and ached over her, and that meant something…didn't it?

It was probably one in the morning or later, I gauged by the moon. I pulled myself up with a sigh and started around the right bank, on up toward the path that led between the lake and the town.

There wasn't a sign of life up ahead, but I knew well enough that our town slept soundly, and that it was close. As I watched for a glimpse of it, thoughts of the lake fell behind, and my chest tightened. The farther I walked, the more I felt like my ribs had been stretched over my heart and did not reach quite far enough.

And then the first rooftop came into view.

My hand went up to my mouth, my fingers digging into my lips. I pushed through the last branches. And there it was.

I could have drawn a picture for you, from memory, and it would have looked exactly the same. The sloping valley with familiar houses—the Whites', the Taylors', the Browns'—the paths curving and intersecting at the barns, the dairy. Just out of sight, I knew, was the vegetable garden, and down below, the town shed. It was like finding treasure, or a fairy tale turned real.

It was also like drowning.

My guts started to churn and I wrapped my arms around the nearest tree, as much for support as to hold on to something real. I shook my head, then leaned it against the knobby bark. I felt feverish and sweaty, like I might faint.

My guts were having a conversation with my brain. My guts said I was not going a step farther. They reminded me of everything that had gone wrong in the town, down in that shed, in the church (the tip of which I could just see over the rise). They said there was no reason for me to be here, that I wasn't supposed to be here, and what's more, that I didn't want to be here. My brain was saying something else entirely. It said I had come all this way. It said this was what I needed to do.

My heart, it seemed, was torn.

It was the thought of my own house—down around the bend to the right, I knew—that got me moving.

Though I was still far from the nearest house, I started forward gingerly, as if the slightest sound might bring somebody running. What would they do if they did see me? I wondered. Yell curses, wake up the rest of the town? Hug me and thank God that I was home? The first option seemed more likely.

Just calm down, Glory. Nobody's going to wake and hop out of their beds because of a few crackling leaves.

I walked slowly, though. Finally I reached the deep, dusty furrow of one of the main paths that I knew led straight through town. If I turned left, I could go to the church. I knew that was where I was headed, eventually. But I turned right, counting the cows out to graze in the lower field as I walked.

One, two, three, four, five...

Then, feeling too agitated by that, I gazed at my feet and counted the steps.

I didn't stop counting until I reached my own front yard. I didn't need to look up to know I was there. The crooked hook in the path where our grass started was more than familiar to me, it was a part of me.

My lips pressed together tight as I lifted my head. My eyes took it in all at once. It was the picture of everything that should have and could have been for me, but wasn't.

I was home, at last.

CHAPTER
ELEVEN

The front yard was as tidy as ever, the well pump sticking up from the grass like a timer in one of those modern, store-bought turkeys. Looking up, I saw the leaded glass of my bedroom window, glinting unevenly. Was it still *my* bedroom window? Had they changed the room by now, to something else? I wasn't sure which possibility was more tragic. I wondered what the Johansens had done with Katie's room. But then, with all those kids they would have probably used the space. Still, it must have been so hard, at first.

I walked up to the front door, as close as I dared. In the morning, Mama and Daddy and the others would be coming in and out of it. They'd come in and out of it *today*. I examined the wood, wanting to touch it but keeping away. I'd forgotten about the heart-shaped rust stain on the doorknob. The door—every-thing about the house—looked smaller than I'd remembered.

Out to the right of the house, there was a big maple that

Mama had planted when I was just a baby. Folks teased her, saying we already had all the trees we could ever want all around us. But Mama had ignored them. She said she knew she'd like the way it looked, once it grew, and of course she had. I slipped away from the door into the shadows of the maple (they seemed so large in the moonlight now that the tree was full grown), padding around the side of the house toward the back.

The back porch was hard to see, what with a small stand of woods reaching right up to the house on the side I was on. But I found it with my feet, squinting until my eyes adjusted and I could see its outline. There, just across the wooden floor, was the washboard, a low hanging clothesline strung above it, all the way back to a tree I knew stood off in the shadows. One piece of clothing hung from the line, swaying slightly in the breeze. I walked over and touched it. Then, curious, I spread it out to see its shape.

Oh. It was a little dress, as high as the washboard maybe, with yellow stripes all down the front. It had to be baby Marie's. How she must have grown!

I couldn't picture her without thinking of her smell, like powder and something softer and cleaner that came just from her. I put my face to her dress. The scent was soapy, but still, like my family, and home. I pulled it off the line, carefully, and sat down where I was, holding it to my eyes. And then, at last, I started to cry.

It was all I could do to keep quiet. I managed it so well and so silently that you could have sat right down next to me and not have heard a thing. I missed them so much! And it was all my cursed fault. I could have done so much differently. I could have done just *one thing* differently.

Finally I rubbed my nose with my sleeve, getting hold of myself but still in misery. Joe had said it had all been an accident. He'd said what got taken away from me was much worse than anything I'd actually done to deserve it. But it wasn't true. If it were, how could I ever survive how unjust it was?

I stood up abruptly, finished. I couldn't stand being here anymore, so close to Mama and Daddy. I hung Marie's dress back up on the line, very carefully. I'd just get a quick look in the window then—

CRASH!

Oh my gosh! What had happened? What had happened?

I swung my head toward the noise, panic-stricken.

There, to the left of my feet, was the culprit. One of Mama's old wash buckets, gone tumbling across the porch.

Cursed Glory. I'd knocked it over with my backpack.

I stood frozen, looking immediately up at the windows, my breath still. No lights went on, the windows stared out darkly like big blind eyes. And then...

No. I thought I'd seen movement, but it must have been a glimmer in the glass. I waited several more minutes, in any case, before I moved one muscle. Finally my breathing returned to normal. I longed to get a closer look into the windows, like I'd planned, but I didn't dare. I stood a moment longer. And then I padded away.

I followed the path toward the church, catching every inch of the view with my eyes. I thanked goodness it was a clear night. Beyond the houses, the fields glowed green until they met the tree line, beautiful as any memory of home I had. I walked past several of our neighbors'. The simple farmhouses were much humbler than the buildings I'd seen in Shadow Tree or Boston, but to me they were gorgeous. It was funny how little had changed since I'd gone, considering how much had changed for me since I'd seen it. Old Mrs. White's house was the only one that seemed to have been altered at all. The front porch drooped, the trim on the windows had become chipped and a little decayed.

Mr. White must be even worse off than he was, I thought as I passed, *to let the house get so dingy. Or else he's dead.* I wrinkled my nose, uncomfortable.

I pictured the Aiden home—how clean it was, how well lit and warm and modern. Compared to where I'd been living, these houses *all* looked a little...*poor.* Not that they weren't dear to me—it's just, they had seemed so big and fine before. Even the Johansens', when I reached it, surprised me. It had been the fanciest house in Dogwood, and even in my memories it had looked huge, and bright white, and elegant—just the way Mrs. Johansen, being an outsider, would have wanted it.

But now, seeing it with fresh eyes, I was touched to think how much Mrs. Johansen must have given up to come here. The house was a little lopsided, and black soot clung in a thick stripe beside the front door, beginning at the ground level. Coal from the stove, I figured, leaking out and up. All over, the paint was a dingy shade of white, nearing gray. There was a large chink worn away in the chimney that it seemed Mr. Johansen would have fixed by now.

Thinking of Katie's daddy, I shivered. I wondered if he had ever told Mrs. Johansen that he'd seen me, back in Boston, and figured probably not. I pictured his eyes, so bloodshot that night, and so angry, when he'd driven me to the abandoned lot. I remembered the smell of spirits on his breath. I couldn't help feeling spooked, and at the same time helpless. In this house were the people I'd hurt the most, and there was nothing I could do to make it better. Mrs. Johansen had always been a friend to me—kind, caring, loving—but I didn't even have the power, or the right, to tell her I was sorry.

Breathing hard, I turned my feet uphill and headed away from the house, on toward the church. As I climbed, the night started to feel heavy to me—and thick. There was this sense of dread inside, like the spring inside me was coiling more tightly than it could go. Looking up as I walked, I could see the building sitting above me—peering down on everything as if it was judging us sinners below, with me being the worst sinner of all.

And here was the proof. About one hundred yards behind the church, in a private, peaceful lot, under three big weeping cherries, was my destination. I walked right past the church, with all its memories of Sundays spent indoors and the night I was cast out, and turned down the short path that I knew led there. To the town cemetery.

The breeze was blowing the trees that stood over it. The shadows of their limbs bounced off the church walls like wild, waving arms. My breath got shallow at the sight of it, and my feet finally slowed.

It was, after all, the reason I'd come.

About four years ago, there was some town interest in enclosing the cemetery with a modest, black iron gate…something to set it apart. As it was, nobody knew where the lot ended and the forest began. The gravestones just popped up every few feet, trailing off into the tree line. But Zeke Brown had said it would take too much time away from other things to build, and Daddy thought it would be too expensive hauling the raw materials from outside. And the idea had been forgotten.

I'd never thought it would matter to me, either way. But now that I approached the gravestones, and saw how they trickled off here and there onto the edge of the woods, I started to panic. What if the one I was looking for was too hard to see? What if it was covered up by the grass and underbrush?

With each new stone I crouched to view, this idea took stronger hold. There was a Levi Brown, a Lily Brown, two Edgar Browns. There was a collection of Smiths and a few Whites. She wasn't here. She wasn't here.

And then. There.

HERE LIES KATHERINE RUTH JOHANSEN

BELOVED DAUGHTER AND SISTER

DIED AT AGE TWELVE

Time stood still. It stopped to let my heart believe my eyes. And then, the spring inside me let go.

Something stronger than I had ever felt poured into every part of my body. My fingers dug at the skin in my palms, as if they had a life of their own. They pressed harder and harder, the nails breaking the skin. Suddenly my legs were crossing under me. My shoulders started to heave. I don't think I could have cried if I'd wanted to, it was so deep inside me.

I was breaking. There were no thoughts of ever standing up again, or even making the effort to breathe. It had to be impossible to feel this bad and not immediately dissolve.

I had never believed. I had never, ever believed. Not the whole way to Boston, or the whole way back. Not really. Otherwise I surely never would have gone. I would have broken like I was doing now.

I curled up on my side and covered my nose and eyes with my hands. I prayed and prayed to sink into the ground beside Katie. There could be miracles like that, maybe. It was worth a try, praying, wasn't it?

I don't know how long I prayed, because time had disappeared. I know it must not have been more than a few minutes.

It would have been longer, had I not heard what I did, from somewhere behind me, out in the grass.

Someone was coming. And I didn't care. I kept my hands over my eyes, I kept lying there. Let them see me. Let them do whatever they wanted with me. I didn't care. I didn't care in the least.

The footsteps approached quickly, and came to rest a few inches in front of me. Through the cracks in my hands, I saw, with little interest, that the person wore women's slippers. And then the back of my neck started tingling, and despite myself, I pulled my hands away, lifted my head, and looked.

And there was my mama standing above me, her brown hair loose and falling down her back. She looked like an angel come to swoop me away.

CHAPTER
TWELVE

In less than an instant my mama was down around me, wrapping me in her arms. I couldn't see, I could hardly breathe, but I could smell her and feel her, and I didn't care if I got smushed to bits, as long as I got to hold on to her.

"Mama!" I sobbed.

She was so silent she could have been a ghost, only she was squeezing the life out of me and kissing me roughly, over and over, on the top of my head.

"Shhhh. Shhh. Baby," she finally whispered. "Glory Bee. I knew it. I knew."

She pulled back from me, her hands moving to either side of my face so we could look each other square in the eyes.

"Knew?" I breathed, my smile so big the tips of my lips could have met the edges of my eyebrows, tears running down into my mouth.

"I knew you'd come back," she said. "I knew you'd…"

She didn't finish, just waved a hand in the air, then hugged me again, then pulled back.

"Look at you," she said, spreading my arms. She gripped my wrists, hard. She looked me up and down as if she were making sure all the parts were there—at first joyfully, then with an air of worry.

"Mama." I took her in at the same time—noticing all sorts of things at once. Her hair had turned gray around the temples. A crease ran down the space between her eyebrows. Her skin sagged just a bit around her mouth. She looked so much *older*.

"Look at you," she said again, shaking her head. "You've grown. Your clothes…" She fingered my V-neck white T-shirt and glanced down at my shorts. "They're nice. They're so…modern."

I tried to imagine how my clothes might look to her eyes, though I'd long since learned to take T-shirts and shorts for granted. Then I remembered that here in Dogwood, at my age, I should have been in a skirt. I hoped Mama didn't judge me badly for it.

"How's—"

"Where—"

We both stopped, started again, then stopped.

"You first," I said, swiping at my dripping nose and desperately fighting the urge to let more tears fall.

"Where have you been all this time?" she asked, urgently. Her hands pulled back and wiped at her own eyes.

I didn't bother wondering where to start. The words just tumbled out of me before she could finish the question. I needed, so much, for her to know.

"I've been so far, Mama. You wouldn't believe it. I've been to Boston, and I worked in a jewelry store, and I met this boy, and I live with, *lived* with these—"

"W-wait," she said, reaching out her hands to stop me. "Boston? How…" She shook her head, clearing it. "How did you leave Dogwood? What happened to you after…the Judgment?" Mama stopped suddenly. "Why in the world would you go to Boston?"

Okay, breathe. We were both so jittery and excited that we'd gotten way ahead of ourselves. If this was ever going to get anywhere, I would have to keep a clear head, and start from the beginning.

"I don't know how to tell you, Mama. But I can try…"

It all rushed out in minutes, nearly one year's worth of life. There was no time to get Mama to see the realness of the Aidens and Shadow Tree and the Kellys and my school in

Boston. Even if we'd had all the time in the world, I could have never got it across so she could understand. But I tried to describe it all as best I could—the cars and stores and movies and all the people, and how they weren't all bad like the Reverend said.

Occasionally, Mama's hand snaked out to touch my knee, or my shoulder, or my cheek. But otherwise she kept agonizingly quiet, until I was done.

And then, the first question she asked took me by surprise. Her eyes grew fearful and kind of wounded. "What's Mrs. Kelly like?"

I let out a big breath. "Mama, I can tell you more, I can tell you all about her. But first you've got to tell me, how is everyone here? How's Daddy?"

"Oh," she said, straightening up and smiling an apology, I guess for keeping me waiting. Some hair had fallen over her left eye, and she pushed it out of the way. Mama was never untidy except when she went to bed. I had always thought that was when she looked the most beautiful.

"They're good, Glory. Real good. Everybody just works as hard as ever, and Marie...you should see her. She goes everywhere now. She's got a mischievous streak a mile wide."

She went on, about how Teresa was to marry Zeke Brown Jr.,

as everyone had expected she would. She told me how Theo and Lizzie Taylor were sweethearts, and how he planned to learn cobbling from her father, maybe one day taking over the job. Marie was walking and talking and carrying on, and had managed to shove peas down Daddy's pants two nights before, as a joke. "She," my mama said, patting my leg, "reminds me so much of you."

We both smiled at this. And then I thought about it. My bottom lip started to tremble.

"She won't turn out like me, will she?" I asked, tears bursting out anew.

"Oh," Mama sighed, "there, there." She wrapped me in her arms again and rocked me back and forth until the tears settled down into hiccups. It was funny, how peaceful she could make me feel, just by holding me. Even as I sat there at Katie's grave, bleary-eyed and ill and guilty as ever, her presence made it so my body could go numb and quiet.

"There, there," she whispered again. "She'll turn out good. All my daughters have turned out good."

"How can you say that?" I breathed. "I'm awful. I'm a terrible, terrible girl. Even God doesn't love me."

"Oh Glory…" She stroked my hair, smiling ever so gently. "I don't know why the Lord chose this harsh road for you. But, dear heart, you're a good girl. I know that. Your daddy knows that. God knows, too."

I shook my head.

"But Katie... It was me that wanted to drink spirits..."

"Oh, hush." Mama's eyes hardened. She stared at me as if she was staring through me. I'd never seen her look so angry. "Do you think you're the first person to break into the town's supply of spirits?"

What? I had to think over the sentence a few times. *What*?

"People have been getting into the spirits from time to time for as long as I can remember. It's the young men, usually. Your daddy, for one. When he was seventeen."

"What?" I had finally found my voice, but my lips kept opening and closing around the one word.

"Oh, of course they wouldn't tell you young folks. Of course they feel bad about it later, and repent. But still..." She focused on me deeply then. "Glory, I won't deny you were a tougher child than most. More mischievous, more stubborn. But you were a child. You still are." She looked me up and down, sadly. "It was an accident, don't you see? You're so much smarter than me, you're sharp as a whip, but even *I* can see it. Can't you?"

I returned my mama's gaze for as long as I could, then lifted my hand to my eyes. I *couldn't* see it. I couldn't believe her. She thought I was a good girl. She said it was an accident. Just like Joe had said.

"I'm so sorry, Mama," I whispered, my tears squeezing between my fingers. "I'm so—"

"I know you are, Glory. Daddy knows you are. The Johansens know you are. Even the Reverend knows you are." She paused, pulling my hand away from my face and looking up at me under her dark eyebrows. "*Katie* knows you are."

I couldn't help my shoulders from shuddering. But Mama held me fast.

"She knows, Glory. Believe me. You can stop saying it. It's time to stop saying it." She stared into my eyes long enough to make sure I'd heard every word. "Only, Glory…" She pulled back and looked at me again, struggling with whatever it was she wanted to say. "You also need to take care of yourself. You don't…look well."

Oh.

I nodded. "I know, Mama. My time's running up, I guess. But don't worry, now that I've seen you—"

Mama jerked. "What do you mean, your time is running up?" I could see that underneath her nightclothes, her chest heaved.

Oh gosh. Poor Mama.

"The poison. Mama. The Water of Judgment. I know it hasn't been a year yet, but I've been real sick, and—"

"Glory." Mama grabbed me around the shoulders so hard it hurt. "Glory, what are you talking about?"

"The poison..." I was so confused, and so scared of the look in Mama's eyes that I started to tremble.

"Glory, don't you know? I thought you must know by now..."

"Know what, Mama?" I felt like I *should* know. I felt bad for not knowing.

Mama put a hand to her forehead and looked heavenward, then looked at me from underneath her thin eyebrows. "Glory, the poison...it's a story. It's a symbol. I didn't..." She shook her head. "All that's in the Water of Judgment is water."

I stared at her for a long moment, maybe a minute or more. My body had floated away, up into the branches.

"No..." I began.

"Yes. Glory, I know it. All the elders do. It's supposed to make you...sick at heart. It means you've died to us. It's like the body and blood at church—it represents death...but it doesn't kill you."

Her eyes were glassy with tears. "I just thought, seeing you here, alive, you knew."

"But…" I couldn't think. Mama wouldn't lie to me, but…it was impossible. Finally I lit on one reason why. "Lance King!"

Mama shook her head again. "Lance King took his own life. He wasn't as strong as you. Being cast out broke his heart."

"But it broke my heart, too!" I cried, not knowing which way on this earth was up or down anymore, or if I was really sitting with my mama at all. What did I know about anything, if I didn't know that I was dying? I wiped at my face, which was completely wet, but still I couldn't stop crying.

"Yes," Mama said, "but you're strong. You're stronger than Lance King was. That's how I knew you'd come back. I knew you'd get through it, and I'd see you again."

I went back to hiccuping, crossing my arms over my stomach. "But, Mama, then how come I'm sick?"

Her eyes met mine, and then slowly traveled down to my left. My own eyes followed.

Here lies Katherine Ruth Johansen

"Could it be," Mama asked, looking like she already knew the answer to the question she would ask, "that the poison did its job, even as well as you thought? Could it be that you *are* sick at heart?"

I thought about drinking the Water of Judgment on the night I was cast out, and how it had tasted like nothing. I remembered the feeling in my stomach whenever I thought about Katie, and how it felt the same as when I was ill. I thought of how the doctors had said they couldn't find anything wrong with me, and how I'd stayed convinced that that could only mean the worst.

And then I fell with my head upon my mama's lap, and cried and cried until all my tears ran out, at last.

CHAPTER
THIRTEEN

The sky was as close as it could be to midnight blue without being quite that light. A brightening had taken place that, if you are a city girl, you might not have noticed. But Mama and I noticed. It was almost time for folks to rise. It was almost daybreak.

I tried to bite down on this question inside me. If I asked it, I had to be ready for what the answer would be. And I knew, deep down, that the answer would be no.

"Mama, can I stay?" I whispered, feeling quieter now that day was coming. "If I'm going to live, can I come live at home?"

Mama didn't answer, but she didn't have to. I've never seen a look more sorry, and at the same time more soothing. Symbols or no, town law was town law.

"You'll be fine," she said. "I know you will. You're a modern girl now," she said, brushing at a dried leaf that had stuck to my sleeve, her voice catching.

"The Johansens?" I asked.

"They're okay, Glory. They're good. You worry about your-self. You've done enough worrying about everyone else."

From the way Mama said it, you'd think I wasn't the selfish girl I'd always thought I was. Maybe I wasn't. Maybe I wasn't anything I'd thought I was.

We stood out in front of the church and held each other for many minutes, not saying a word. I kept thinking, *I can hold on just a few more seconds, a few more, a few more*. But finally we pulled apart. My mama had circles under her eyes, and she looked exhausted.

"Maybe you can rest a bit today?" I asked.

She smiled. "Oh, you know better than that."

Of course I knew. Mama would be at her chores from dawn to dusk. It is a hard life, in Dogwood, on top of being a pure and simple and happy and safe one. But it wasn't *my* life anymore.

Mama kissed my cheek one more time, softly. "Now you'll want to go through the main gate. It's about a two-hour walk to the paved road, and Lord knows how far to the nearest civilized place." She jokingly rolled her eyes at the word *civilized*. I'd rarely ever gotten to see my mama's sense of humor, and I smiled, appreciating it now.

"You be good," she said. And before I could say another word, her back was to me and she was rushing away, her shoulders hunched up tight and her hand to her throat.

Lord, it hurt. I fought the urge to follow after her. I looked up at the sky and found myself asking God to help ease the ache. I walked out to the front of the church to see her disappearing down the hill.

When she was gone, I turned in a half circle, gazing around. Something caught my eye.

Squinting, I stepped closer to get a better look. Sunk slightly in the soil along the side wall, looking forlorn and abandoned, was a red clay planter. It had clearly been tossed out here, out of the way, maybe to be cleaned out and reused another day.

But…

I walked right up to it and knelt down to examine the plant, and my breath caught. Forget-me-nots. It was the planter that had sat at the front of the church, the night I was cast out. The flowers that Katie had nursed so well. That they were still blooming, out here with no one to care for them, was a miracle.

I caressed the leaves and the delicate petals of the flowers, reflecting. These flowers had been left to die, twice. I'd given up on them once and, apparently, so had the Reverend…or whoever had dumped them here. But they were still growing and flourishing. They were still holding themselves up to the light, surviving despite everything and everyone.

I wrapped my hands under the base and lifted the planter up. I couldn't just leave it here, alone like this, ready to be thrown away. I tightened my grip and headed back down the main path into the center of the village—knowing where it belonged.

The Johansens' house was still dark and quiet, its windows blank. The front porch, where Mrs. Johansen always liked to sit and do chores, where the Johansen boys often hung off the banisters, was bare but for one rocking chair, and cleanly swept. My first step sounded loud on the wooden stair, so I let only the tips of my shoes touch the rest of the way, up, up to the wooden door. Gentle as a dove, I laid the planter down at its foot.

I didn't count on Mrs. Johansen knowing who it was from. She probably wouldn't, though she might guess, if she read my mama's eyes.

It was the only thing I could think to give her. And it wasn't because it was me I wanted her to remember, or Katie, who, of course, she would remember always, in a million ways, every day. It was this idea that hope grows. That maybe Katie was gone for a little while, but not forever. That maybe in the bigger picture, Katie was just waiting to rebloom in some other way.

I didn't expect Mrs. Johansen or anybody else to see all of this meaning in a pot of flowers. But I hoped she would at least look at them with the tiniest bit of happiness. That, I figured, was the most I could ask.

Veering left, I made for the tree line on the lower end of our valley, where I'd be more obscured on my way toward the gate. It was early yet, but already, I knew, folks were stirring in their beds, or up and putting on the coffee, cooking eggs, getting dressed. Only, now that I thought of these things, my feet went the opposite way at the trees, once again carrying me toward my own house.

My heart skipping all about, I snuck into the back, nestling myself deep in the bushes—but not so deep that I couldn't see… What had I come to see? Of course I knew.

In the kitchen, my mama was already at the stove. I could tell by the way she moved her arms that she was making bis-cuits, though I couldn't see her hands. A figure with long black hair appeared behind hers. Teresa. Her face was far away, and a little hard to see through the glass, but from what I could tell, she was as pretty as ever, and flushed, and happy. I bit my lip. That was okay. That was good. I wanted her to be happy.

There was more motion in the background. My stomach

turned. It had to be Daddy or Theo. I strained to see, but whoever it was stayed beyond Teresa, just out of clear sight. If they just…

Minutes went by, but everyone seemed to have disappeared from the kitchen. They were surely at the table, eating. I moved farther on, to the left of the house, and forward a bit, so I could just get a glimpse of the water pump out front. When Daddy and Theo came out, they'd have to come out this way.

A squeak and a rumble—the sound of the front door opening—and then I heard their footsteps. Theo appeared first, bending over the pump, getting a few big gulps of water. Great day! He was even taller than he'd ever been, and there seemed to be more to him. He wasn't fat, just more like…a grown-up. His face was tanned and stubbly looking. He was very manly, I noted with pride.

Daddy was behind him, waiting for a turn at the water, patiently for once. He wore his overalls, his hair the usual mess. His big hands rested on his waist, but I couldn't see his face until he turned and looked up toward the barn lot, showing me his profile. It looked exactly the same—no new wrinkles, no shock of gray like Mama had. Daddy was strong; I didn't think I'd ever meet anybody stronger. It would take a lot to bring him down. I felt happiness and regret to know my leaving hadn't.

I drank the sight of him in, my heart in my throat. I wanted to run to him. I almost did. But knowledge of what was right and wrong kept my feet planted.

He seemed to linger now, surveying the landscape, as if a day of chores didn't lay ahead of him and he had all the time in the world. The expression on his face was curious.

Then it happened. It was only for a second or two, but when I think about it now, over and over, it lasts much longer, and I always ask myself, *Did he? Or didn't he?*

He turned all the way around, facing straight toward me and, for one blessed moment, seemed to meet my eyes. I froze among the bushes, holding my breath and staying stock-still. I wasn't sure if he'd seen me or not.

He only stared for a second, and in that time he did nothing to acknowledge me—no smile, or wave, or even a frown. The only thing he did was, as he turned back away, he nodded, a move so small it was almost nothing. And then, without looking back, he walked up the hill.

I watched him go, afraid that my lungs were going to get the better of me, and force the sound out of my mouth. A moan. *I* was a moan—my whole body was a moan, at losing my daddy, and mama, and brother and sisters, and this place, and everything I used to know. But I managed to hold it in, like someone much older and wiser. *I guess*, I thought, *I am a grown woman, Daddy. I guess that I'll be going.*

The woods took me straight up to the town gate, and by the time I'd gotten there, I hadn't seen one person, outside of my family. But just in case, I'd crouched and held my breath almost the whole way. Even when I reached the gate, and ducked around it, I feared that any minute I might be seen from behind, and caught. But then I was fifty feet away. And then a hundred. And still I walked as softly as I could until, when I looked over my shoulder, I could see no sign of the gate, or the town, behind me.

And then, when I was sure no one was going to see me, I stood up straighter, and I took a deep breath. I took big steps. And I walked faster, and faster, and faster.

It was high noon before I reached the gasoline station. Sweat had gathered on the tiny crease above my lips, and I rubbed at it with my fingertips. If I hadn't been walking so fast, the breeze would have kept me cool. Up here in the mountains today, fall was most definitely in the air.

A car breezed past. "*Too little, too late,*" I muttered, thinking of my long walk, during which I'd seen not one. But it didn't matter. The vista from the gasoline station was long and wide, showing me the road winding down one hill and up another. Beyond that final rise were rolling hills, green and dark green with kale and alfalfa, yellow with dried up cornstalks, watercress, goldenrod. The Appalachians rose up around and behind it all, beautiful, precious, and close to my heart. I'd been hurrying to get here, to reach the telephone and make an important call. But now I stopped, and took it all in.

Somewhere down in front of me, Shadow Tree had been waiting for a long time, for me to come back. Becky and her husband, Amelia and the boys, the Rock Shop, a life. It was all there for the taking, should I live, like Mama said I would.

I thought of Boston, and the Kellys. No brothers, no sisters. No normal teenage life. There was Joe, but no Becky. There was contentment, but no life like I'd imagined.

I walked through the glass doors of the station. A man with a fluorescent green cap stood behind the counter, watching the television mounted on a side wall. I didn't feel shy going up to him. Not even about asking him if I could have some change for a dollar to make a phone call. I laid one of my last five dollars on the counter, and he pushed the coins back at me. Then I turned to the little booth with the pay phone, deposited enough change, plucked the phone off its hook, and dialed the number I'd memorized by heart.

A woman's voice answered.

"Hello?" I said, nervously, sheepishly. I thought about Becky and her music and her laugh and her kindness, and my dear, dear mountains. But I didn't feel a second's hesitation. "Hello, Mrs. Kelly, it's Glory," I said. "I'm ready to come home."

EPILOGUE

Have you ever been to the Appalachian mountains? Have you ever watched the sun rise over a West Virginia mountain lake, making steam come off the water like smoke?

Have you ever been a bad person? Have you ever been lost? Have you ever thought you were alone, and found out you were wrong?

I have.

But these days, I am never alone. Not since the Kellys showed up at that gas station in West Virginia to take me home to Boston. Even when they're out, I am on the telephone to one of my friends, Sadie or Joe or even Becky Aiden.

Even when I'm alone, I am still not alone. Having people that love you makes that impossible, I reckon. Being adopted, I know even surer than most that I'm wanted, day after day. At least, that's how it seems to me.

Not that I don't get lonely sometimes. I miss Mama and Daddy still, all the time. The Kellys are my second family, but they'll never be my first. I like to picture the Mason kids growing and changing, turning into adults—Teresa as a mama herself, Theo getting married, baby Marie a smaller version of me, feisty and stubborn, ready to say no to dresses when the time comes. It makes me sad, to think of it—them all getting older without me. Mama and Daddy will be grandparents someday, and I won't be there to see it.

Joe says that's hooey, that they'll come around and visit me sometime. That I may never go to Dogwood again, but bits of Dogwood—the most important bits—will come to me. He says it's a dying way of life, that by the time Marie is old enough, she'll strike out on her own, too, like me, only for happier reasons.

I don't know. Like I've told Joe a million times, he doesn't *know* Dogwood. But I let him talk me into things all the same. For instance, I've started sending letters home, every couple of weeks. I never asked my mama if the one I sent ever arrived, and it's one of my biggest regrets. But I don't dwell on it. I just send them, and hope. Joe says if the Reverend or anybody else doesn't like it, they can stick it up their noses. He is a boy after my own heart. Which is a good quality in a boyfriend. We'll be going together for a year come August.

That's right, a year! Which means, of course, that since I'm writing this, I haven't died yet, and I don't plan to. Anytime soon, at least. Of course, when it's your time to go, you've gotta go, but until that day comes I'm not worrying about it. I'm too busy living my big modern life. Movies, gardening, reading, going to school, sometimes just sitting quietly with the Kellys, watching *Jeopardy!* I'm lucky to be doing any of it, and I try not to forget it. God knows I can be foolish sometimes, and forget to appreciate all my luck and all my blessings.

To tell the truth, I'm not sure if it's luck or blessings that's gotten me so far. I've been thinking a lot about God. I've been thinking Joe's right, that God's not this old guy with a beard who is watching and listening every second, making sure we don't mess up, punishing us for the dumb mistakes we make. I like to picture God more like the air, something that's so deep and mysterious it doesn't even have a shape.

But whether or not I'm right about that, I know I'm right about this: All that time I was a black hole inside, and all that time I felt unloved and lost and pure miserable, I was headed somewhere. I was headed here. I'm like a pair of needles making a pattern out of yarn, but it's one I can't see. And that's fine. The important thing is that somebody is doing the knitting. I just know it.

And whoever and wherever they are, I know that Katie is with them, and smiling.

*Don't miss the other books
in this gripping drama:*

WITHDRAWN